Top Model

Estelle Li and the September Issue

Adam Jay Ung

advice. The content within this book has been derived from various sources. Please consult a licensed professional before attempting any techniques outlined in this book.

By reading this document, the reader agrees that under no circumstances is the author responsible for any losses, direct or indirect, that are incurred as a result of the use of the information contained within this document, including, but not limited to, errors, omissions, or inaccuracies.

Table of Contents

Disclaimer

This is a work of fiction. Names, characters, businesses, events, and incidents are the products of the author's imagination. Any names, places, or events that have resemblance to actual persons, actual places, or actual events are used fictionally and have no association to its real-life namesake. The opinions expressed are those of the characters and should not be confused with the author's.

Prologue

The camera flashed without pause, while her eyes remained unblinking. She stood regal, powerful, and confident, as all top models are thought to be.

Her nose was petite, her almond-shaped eyes deeply determined, and her small lips firmly set. She had the ability to stare into every soul watching her through the lens of a camera or through the pages of Vogue magazine.

She stood before tumbles of dramatic red drapes and commanded the spotlight while shouldering the weight of an equally theatrical and billowing red dress. Swathed in the heavy silk, she gave the camera a thousand poses a minute. With every move she made, the fabric of her fashion flowed about her eight-inch heels and licked at the feet of the matching Victorian couch perched behind her, awaiting her inevitable collapse.

It is believed that the face of a Chinese fashion model in America is a diverse, but pure, beauty.

In the Western world, Asian beauty is seen as equally alien and flawless. Yet, although stereotyped to be perfectionists, one model's efforts towards achieving perfection is more earthly than anyone could possibly imagine...

Chapter 1:

Estelle Li

As morning graced the city of New York, Estelle Li's eyes fluttered open. While she was a 20-year-old Chinese American, she looked 14 in her innocent and sleepy state. Remnants of her dream, of red drapes and blinding white flashes, played through her mind as she simmered to consciousness.

Her eyes were absentmindedly glued to the foggy window of her apartment that overlooked the dirty yet bustling street below. Watching rain droplets create patterns against the glass pane, she sighed and turned over in her bed. Her phone lay face down on her bedside table, and she reached over to grab it. The digital clock on the bright screen told her it was 8:05 a.m.

Immediately, she swiped her finger down to check her notifications, which were dominated by her Instagram page. After briefly scrolling through the app, she locked her phone and put it back down next to a pile of iconic Vogue magazines she'd stacked perfectly on the small table. At the top was one from 1996—the September issue that featured Amber Valletta and Kate Moss.

She gave the cover girls a small good morning smile before pulling herself out of bed and into her bathroom. Her small apartment was clean and neat, but cozy. It bordered on minimalistic with gray tones throughout, broken by the warmth of a few beiges and wooden accents. Her bathroom was adjacent to her bedroom with the doorway nestled in between ceiling height closets. On the white counter stood an array of pricey facial care and makeup products, all lined up in order of her specific skin-care routine.

Estelle looked at herself in the wide mirror and grabbed her toothbrush. While brushing, she stepped on her scale: 110 lbs.

Not bad… but not where I need to be.

With her toothbrush still in her mouth and foam around her lips, she stood with her back against the door where she'd marked up measurements: 5'7". As if she'd expected her height to change overnight, she sighed. She wasn't as tall as the top fashion models were expected to be. Next, she grabbed her tape measure and checked her chest, waist, and hip measurements: 34-24-34. She was the perfect size by any of the world's standards—except in the fashion industry.

I might as well be a whale...

In her small kitchen, with similar white countertops and touches of timber throughout, she poured herself her usual black coffee and quickly made an omelet. While she ate, she checked her phone again, before cleaning up and getting dressed into leggings and a sports bra.

Next on her morning routine, she practiced her runway strut. She'd positioned a full-length mirror in her living room, with a clear pathway dedicated to her practices. She pulled on her six-inch-tall pumps, and walked up and down the pathway 20 times, working up a sweat. Like clockwork, she turned and sat down on the couch to replace her heels with socks and running shoes—because next, she would go to the gym.

Her gym was only a short walk from her apartment building, about two blocks. When searching for a place she could actually afford with the little money she made, she was lucky to come across her tiny one-bedroom apartment squashed into a corner at the top of a five-story building. It was a cramped lifestyle but as long as she was in the city and could practice her catwalk in her living room, she was happy.

In the cardio room, Estelle puffed as she ran on the treadmill. Her body was dripping with sweat before she slowed to a walking cool down and stepped off. She'd run five miles. In the weight room, she worked on her chest and shoulders for 20 minutes, ending her workout.

Back in her kitchen, a still-sweaty Estelle made herself an açai bowl, topped off with a large spoon of peanut butter—her favorite indulgence. After a steamy shower, she measured herself again, with no changes. Sighing, she wiped the mist from her mirror and started her extensive skin-care regimen.

Finally ready for the day, Estelle dressed in a black bodysuit, black skinny jeans, and a pair of sneakers. She threw a bottle of water into her oversized tote bag which already contained her comp cards, iPad, gum, peanut buttery snacks, makeup, sunscreen, a hat, a sweater just in case, and her high heels. She then headed out the door and walked down the noisy street while checking her phone. There was a message waiting that caused her mouth to lift in a small smile.

Sam: Good luck on your casting :)

Estelle: Thanks <3

She arrived at the designated building in the heart of Manhattan, and noted the sign on the street door:

CASTING: M.L.B. F/W 2021 SHOW

She headed inside and changed into her heels while she waited with the rest of the models. When her name was called, she breathed in steadily and walked into the casting room with confidence. This was her job and her passion; this was what all her routines and hard work were for. Before every casting she attended, she reminded herself of this.

She saw three designers sitting behind a table and smiled widely before putting her comp card down in front of them. They didn't greet her with words, only a slight nod of the head and a small smile. She handed her iPad to the designer on the left, who gratefully took it and began swiping through her digital portfolio.

They were Miya Murakami, Luna Windsor, and Blakeson Young. They had an assistant, Amelia, who sat to the side and looked on with her pen in hand. While Estelle stood waiting, they whispered amongst themselves about her measurements. While this was normal, it was always an awkward and uncomfortable moment. Blakeson suddenly looked up and smiled tightly.

"Would you mind showing us your walk?"

Estelle nodded. "I'll do whatever it takes." *Joking, not joking,* she thought nervously.

Everyone smiled at that, and Luna replied. "Great. Whenever you're ready."

Her face became serious, and she strutted up to them before turning and heading back to her original position. As she did so she felt her stomach churn into a ball of nerves. It didn't scream *spectacular.* It was nothing special. It had no *wow* factor. She could feel it in her bones, and she could feel their judgment in her tightened chest.

"Thanks," Miya was next to speak. "Do you mind if we just take your measurements?"

"Of course," Estelle replied and stepped out of her heels. Amelia, the assistant, quickly jumped up and took her height and torso measurements.

"5'7"… and 34-24-34."

Miya nodded and looked at Estelle. "Thank you." She circled the numbers on Estelle's comp card, and added it to a pile, face down. To Estelle, it felt like a nail in her coffin.

She forced a smile. "Thank you for seeing me." With that, she turned and walked towards the doorway, where the next model stood in wait. *So, I'm not getting this gig,* she thought to herself as she stuffed her heels back into her bag and donned her sneakers again. Completely deflated, she swung the exit door open and left the building.

***

Steam filled the air as carts with metal dishes of dumplings were pushed about the restaurant by elderly Asian women. Estelle sat with her parents, Richard and May Li, as they ate dim sum together. They were Chinese immigrants from Cambodia, and Richard never let her forget the struggles they endured to get to America, where she and her sister were born.

"Have you check-uh your email this morning?" Richard asked her, his Chinese accent thick.

"Yeah, why?" Estelle asked, looking down and picking at her food. Her mother sat quietly, eating her dumplings and watching them. She couldn't speak a lick of English, but she could follow along with their conversation. Richard leaned forward and spoke to Estelle.

"This morning, I sent you a job posting I find on LinkedIn dot com."

"I saw it."

"And?" he asked after a brief pause.

Sighing, Estelle looked up at him. "Do we have to do this every time we see each other?"

"You have been trying to do the modeling for four years now. How much longer are you going to pursue that? You still work at restaurant—"

"Only part-time. Modeling is already more than a full-time job. If I'm gonna pursue my dream I need to be fully committed."

Her father looked at her pointedly. "When I was young, my father would never allow me to pursue my dream. He say only A-B-C kid pursue they dream. It's uh-so-selfish. They don't care about taking care of they family, you know? Get a real job, and you can have fun on the weekend with the money you earn. Understand what I'm talkin' 'bout?"

"Yeah… but that's an old, outdated, Asian way of thinking about life."

Ever since Estelle was a child, her Asian heritage had clashed with her understanding of American culture. At school she'd see her American friends' parents praise them for every little achievement, only to go home to a father who asked her why she was graded a B and not an A on her report. She realized long ago that Asians focused on competition, on getting ahead, while Americans were more pleasure-orientated—that which brought you the most happiness was what you would do. Her friends played soccer for fun, while her father forced her to play the piano.

She wasn't ungrateful; she knew that her determination and drive to be the best came from exactly that type of strict, authoritarian upbringing. She just wished he would see the effort she put in and support her ambitions a little more.

Richard didn't appreciate her comment and shot her a look. "He is right! If I pursue my dream at your age, we would not be here now eating good food. We be on the street. Homeless! You should at least have a second option. It's not too late to go back to school."

Estelle frowned at him. "Did Bill Gates or Mark Zuckerberg have a backup plan? They found passion in one thing and pursued it. They were both Harvard dropouts, but they've changed the world."

"If you want to go into technology or engineering industry, I be proud. That's a more respeck-uh-table career than model. How do model change the world like Microsoft or Facebook? If you can show me, maybe I support."

She gave up arguing and took his words in as she continued to pick at her food. Her mom noticed the tension and spoke softly in Mandarin.

"You're so skinny… Eat more."

She grabbed a pork bun with her chopsticks and dropped it into Estelle's plate, who sighed as she looked at the food she knew she shouldn't be eating.

***

Estelle's part-time job was waitressing at a high-end Italian restaurant called Tomato Basil. She had a shift after meeting her parents and arrived wearing her uniform: black pants and a white button-up. She quickly wrapped her apron around her waist before getting started. It was a busy place and she found herself running between tables and the kitchen the entire evening.

At a table with a group of middle-aged men, she took their finished plates from them along with the check. "Thank you." She smiled at them, as was in her job description. Closing out their check, she counted her tips for the night—$375.

Eh, not great, she thought with disappointment.

"I'm so hungry." The voice of her fellow server and boyfriend, Sam Yang, came from behind her. She turned around as he was pulling his apron off. She smiled and watched him. He was also Chinese, tall and lanky, with black hair that was always just a tad too long, but he had one of those faces that immediately told you he was a nice guy.

"Me too," she replied and they made their way to the kitchen.

They headed outside to the alleyway behind Tomato Basil, where they sat down on a pair of yellow crates with slices of what was considered the best pizza in the district. Estelle had a tissue in hand and dabbed at the oil on her slice.

Brushing her hair behind her ear, Sam watched her. "Just enjoy the grease babe… It's part of the flavor."

She shook her head. "I needa lose inches."

"I gotta say, personally, I like you a little chubbier. Makes my little chubby a little chubbier, if you know what I mean."

He leaned in and pretended to gnaw at her neck while she giggled happily.

"Stop, stop, stop! The other day I found a study that showed a 35 calorie reduction when you do this, which is about 13 percent of the total calories per slice."

"Wow… A whole 35. *So much…*"

"Hey, every calorie counts, okay? I wanna be on the cover of Vogue one day, not working here all my life."

"Wait, this isn't your dream job?" Sam asked with a confused face.

"Shut up!" Estelle laughed at him. "Hey, seriously. Do you ever regret going to college when you could've spent that time and money pursuing a dream?"

He stared into the distance and thought for a moment. "I don't know… I've never had dreams of being famous or anything like that."

"No, but everybody dreams of something bigger and better for themselves."

"Well, when I was in college, I just wanted to finish so my parents wouldn't gimme crap. I mean, you know how it is."

"How what is?"

"You think Asian parents are proud of their kids. for simply graduating college?" He shook his head. "That's an expectation they have of you as soon as you leave the womb. So if I didn't at least finish, they would've never let me live it down. I mean, they still ask me every week, *do you found job yet?*" He lifted his finger in mockery of his parents, but Estelle wasn't laughing now.

"That doesn't bother you?"

He shrugged. "I have a job. Just not one they think is *respectable*." He hooked his fingers simultaneously in the air to indicate that their definition of respectable was relative. "What's crazy to me is that they expect their kids to know what they plan to do with the rest of their lives by the time they're 16."

"I did."

Sam looked at his feet, taking her words in. "Well... that's 'cause you're you and I'm not. So..."

An awkward silence passed as he shrugged, and Estelle noticed his discomfort about the topic. She sighed and tried to swivel the focus to her parents instead.

"I'm pretty sure my dad thinks of me as a failure... He still doesn't talk about me to his friends. But he's always so proud of Christian, though. '*You should be more like your younger sister. Going to Columbia to study economic.*'" Sam chuckled as she mimicked her father's voice. She smiled but shook her head. "It's as if he believes that constantly repeating this is gonna make me jealous and inspire me to go back to school or something."

He moved to brush his knee against hers and looked into her eyes meaningfully. "You know how many Asian parents can tell their friends that their kid is studying economics in college? How many of them can say that their daughter's a top fashion model?"

Estelle considered his words, although she wasn't convinced. "But I'm not a top model. I still work here. You know, I was thinking the other day... I can't ever remember a time when my dad's told me he was proud of me. All he ever tells me is I should go back to school.”

“Because education is a path to a traditional career. A career leads to money and money equals success. Everything's about money. Money makes Asians feel proud.”

Sam shrugged simply; he had a very straightforward way of thinking. He didn't need to overanalyze his life, he just wanted to live it. But Estelle needed answers and continued on about her father's disapproval.

“What my dad doesn't realize is that if I become a top model, I could make more money than he ever did in all his years working for Deloitte... combined!”

“Well, hey, tell you what, if you're looking for a quick and easy way to the top, the casting couch is always right around the corner. Just saying...”

“Shut up! I'd never do that. Can you imagine someone telling you, *Your daughter blew her way to the top. Aren't you proud of her?*”

Sam thought about it before answering. “I mean, I'd be okay with it as long as they say she was the best they've ever had... 'cause that's at least an achievement.”

Estelle gasped and smacked his arm while he laughed loudly. “Gross!”

“I'm kidding! In all seriousness, I think if your dad saw you on a giant billboard in Times Square, or on the

cover of Vogue—even if you haven't made it rich yet—
he couldn't help but be proud of you. And his friends
will probably be the ones talking about you."

She chuckled and shook her head as she finished
dabbing her pizza, then peeled half the cheese off and
put it onto Sam's slice. Under her breath, she muttered,
"That'll be the day…" while Sam happily chomped
down on the extra cheese and spoke with his mouth
full.

"You're missing out on some of the best things in life."

Estelle scoffed as she took a bite of her half-naked
pizza.

Chapter 2:

Ford Models

In the morning, Estelle sleepily stepped on her scale, noting her 110 lbs. With her toothbrush in mouth, she measured her torso: 34-24.5-34.5—she'd gained a half-inch around her waist and hips. She immediately spat the toothpaste from her mouth, hearing the toothbrush clatter against the sink as her widened eyes looked at the numbers on the tape measure again.

"Wait, what?"

She tensed with absolute frustration and stomped through her apartment as she went about her morning routine. However, when she took the carton of eggs from the fridge for her morning omelet, she thought twice about it and settled with a cup of black coffee for breakfast instead.

***

After a short subway ride and a brisk walk through the city streets, Estelle arrived to meet with her agent at the Ford Models Agency on 57th Street where the Women's Division was headquartered. Lily Atteberry was a 45-year-old ex-model who knew the business inside and out. She was tall and elegant with silky smooth blonde hair that tumbled over her shoulders and somehow always looked like she'd just left the salon.

When Estelle walked in through the foyer, she glanced at the wall of comp cards lining the hallway to the agents' office—every model Ford represented was up there, including herself.

In the open-plan office, there was a long wooden table where the agents each had a section to themselves. Above their sections were the headshots of the models they represented, and Estelle saw her own right above Lily's head as she sat on the phone.

Noticing Estelle, she quickly covered the mouthpiece and whispered loudly, "Wait for me out on the patio! I'll be there in five minutes."

She gestured towards the patio and Estelle nodded with a quick smile before walking through the room and out the patio door. As she stepped out, the Manhattan skyline appeared before her.

She pulled out her phone and shot a video of the breath-taking view before turning and capturing herself smiling sweetly in the frame with the high-rises behind her. As she sat down on the outdoor sofa, she opened Instagram and posted it to her story with the caption: *On top of the world… or just NYC for now* <3. She checked her notifications: 158 new likes and 33 new followers. Her total followers were 21K, with no blue verification check mark next to her name.

This is good… Estelle thought, reassuring herself. She was getting more and more attention each day with every new post she made. But it wasn't nearly enough for the kind of modeling career she longed for. She needed more exposure and more social media coverage.

After looking up to check if Lily had finished her call yet, she quickly searched for the name "Sofie Tsai." Sofie was an Asian model like Estelle, except only eighteen years old and already much more successful. On her Instagram profile, she had three million followers and a blue verification, as well as five different modeling agencies listed that represented her. Her most recent post was a photo of her on the runway for a Marc Jacobs show, with a Getty Images watermark across the image.

She sat solemnly scrolling through the rest of Sofie's page, longing for the day when she would be as popular and successful. *One day, Stelle… One day soon!*

"Glad you could make it." Lily's voice pulled Estelle from her thoughts and she locked her phone to stand up and hug her. She'd been Estelle's agent for the four years she'd been with Ford so far, so naturally over the years they developed a close friendship. As they sat down across from each other, Estelle answered Lily with a warm smile.

"Hey! Of course."

"How's Sam? Tell him I said hello."

"Yeah, he's good. I will." Estelle continued smiling but was more interested to know about her recent casting.

"So, I heard back from M.L.B."

"Oh yeah?"

"Don't be discouraged by this…"

Estelle nodded slowly, but immediately felt her heart drop. *This doesn't sound promising…*

Lily watched her carefully as she explained, "Because that casting was for runway, they wish you were a little taller. You also need to work on your walk and lose a few inches. Especially on your waist and hips."

"So, you're saying I got the job…" Estelle said sarcastically, trying to mask the disappointment she felt underneath.

"I can only lead you to their doors. It's on you to walk through them. Literally. But in order to do that, it's gonna require molding and adapting to their needs."

Estelle frowned, she knew that she would do whatever she needed to for her career, but it irked her that there was *so much* she was being asked to do, all the time. She thought about her childhood icons, and what they might have gone through.

"You think designers ever told the "Big Six" they needed to lose inches?"

Lily shook her head calmly, having heard similar questions from many young models before. "Everyone's been told to lose inches. Even the '90s supermodels." She paused to think about how to advise Estelle going forward. "But fashion was just so different back then. Editorial and runway work aren't even the only routes models can take anymore. You can get your face out there and make great money doing promotional work, modeling, endorsing a brand on Instagram now. So, remember not to post anything that highlights a brand or a product without talking to me about it first. I might be able to get you paid for those. Have you ever considered that?"

"Instagram modeling?" Estelle asked with disdain as she felt her heart sink.

"No, that's not what I'm saying. There's a difference between being an Instagram model and being a real model who uses Instagram as a platform to get paid to post and promote things on their profile."

"I'd rather be called a porn star than an Instagram model. I seriously can't stand the term 'influencer.'"

"Well, I don't represent porn stars or Instagram models because they're not real models… Got it?"

Estelle nodded. She felt Lily's encouragement but couldn't shake the small feeling of dread growing in her stomach. She wanted to be a supermodel—a top model. And she would do whatever she needed to, to get there. She considered the runway job at hand, and a question came to her mind.

"Is Sofie Tsai gonna be in the M.L.B. show?"

"You know, we don't represent her."

Estelle nodded, somewhat impatiently. She knew Ford didn't represent Sofie, but she also knew that Lily always had insider information. "Did they book her?"

Lily sighed with a nod of her head. "I heard Sofie's in the show."

"Do you consider her a supermodel?"

She thought about it before answering. "I think she's on her way."

Estelle knew this, but it was another thing to hear it from her agent—a professional who knew what she was talking about. It was as if Lily had confirmed her fears. She felt left behind, like Sofie was always there first, booking every job Estelle had longed for. Lily saw Estelle's dejected expression and changed the subject.

"Listen, focus on yourself. Take care of your body, your skin, and work on your walk. Next time I see you I wanna hear that you've lost inches, okay?" Estelle nodded and they stood to hug each other again. "I'll send you all the info right now for your next Go-See on Wednesday. It's for GAP, and from what I'm hearing, it's gonna be shot by Frankie D."

Estelle froze. "Frankie D.? *The* Frankie D.? He just shot last month's cover of Vogue."

"And Bazaar, so yes, *that* Frankie D. Working with him could be huge for you if it goes well."

"Oh my God…"

Lily smiled, sensing that she'd given Estelle something to look forward to and work hard for. She squeezed her shoulder supportively. "Love you. Talk soon!"

***

Back in her apartment, Estelle strode up and down her makeshift runway. The news about a possible GAP shoot with *the* Frankie D. had her feeling determined to do whatever was necessary. At that moment, she wanted to bag the M.L.B. runway show, and Lily had told her to work on her walk, so there she was—doing what needed to be done. Before starting she watched a few videos of iconic runway shows on YouTube as motivational research and resolved to get her walk to perfection.

After what felt like an hour, she'd walked up and down her living room 100 times. Dripping with sweat and feeling her heart pounding against her chest, she sat down on her couch and winced in pain.

Oh, no. What was that sharp pain?

Feeling dread, she carefully removed her heels and a sweltering red blister revealed itself on the bunion area of her right foot. She saw another on her left Achilles heel.

"Shit…" she said, closing her eyes and taking a few deep breaths, trying to soothe her pain. She couldn't deal with setbacks right now. If she wanted to get the shoot with Frankie D., she had to push through the pain and manage whatever came her way. She opened her eyes again and looked up at her wall of inspiration.

She'd put up various photographs and magazine clippings of models and shoots that inspired her. There were Vogue covers and iconic shots of the '90s supermodels like Kate Moss and Jenny Shimizu. She also added a few motivational sayings like, "Keep Calm and Lose Weight," and the infamous quote by Kate Moss, "Nothing tastes as good as skinny feels."

She felt a burning desire to be as great as they were, but first, she needed to deal with the issue at hand. She covered her blisters with bandages, pulled on the thickest socks she had, followed by her running shoes, and hastily headed out the door.

At the gym, she pushed through the stabbing pains of her blisters as she ran on the treadmill. She grimaced when she slowed to her usual walking cool down and noted that she'd run six miles. Estelle then worked her glutes, pushing herself past her usual limits as the sweat trickled down her face.

Later on in her own bathroom, the room filled with steam as she took her time in the shower, using exactly the right amount of her skin-care products in the suggested order. When she turned the water off, she glanced down and saw red liquid swirling down the drain. The hot water had opened her blisters again and they were actively bleeding.

With a frustrated groan, she sat down on the toilet and held a towel to the open sores before reapplying new bandages. She stood and went about her measurements as usual. She weighed 110lbs and measured 34-24.5-34.5. There were no improvements whatsoever.

***

That evening, while on a break from work, Estelle and Sam sat on their crates in the alleyway. Sam was munching happily on a delicious-looking pasta dish from the kitchen, while Estelle puffed on a cigarette and watched a video on her phone. It was titled, *Instagram Models vs Supermodels.*

With her eyes glued to the screen and her cigarette between her fingers, she smirked as the video compared models. Sam looked up from his own phone with a mouth full of pasta.

"You're not hungry?"

"Going back to the gym again tonight. Don't wanna cramp."

He nodded his understanding and looked back down at his phone. Estelle took a long, deep drag of her smoke as she looked down at his video. He was watching a

YouTube video of a gamer speed racing through the original NES's Mario III.

She thought for a moment before asking, "So… Have you been looking for a new job lately?"

Sam's eyes didn't leave his screen as he answered nonchalantly, "Not really."

"I mean, this job is great if it's a means to an end, but—"

"Stelle, are you being an old Asian parent to me right now?"

She frowned and pulled back. "Really? I just want better things for you. You shouldn't be content—" Stopping herself, she shook her head, deciding not to go down that road. "Whatever…" She sighed and put out her cigarette before standing and heading back inside. Sam looked up from his phone and watched her leave.

"I was joking…"

***

After her shift at Tomato Basil, Estelle was back at the gym. She sprinted on the treadmill for a full seven miles before slowing down and grabbing the handrails to steady herself. She closed her eyes for a moment as lightheadedness overtook her.

On a nearby bench, she removed her shoes to check on her blisters—which were evidently open once again as the bandages had slipped off from the sweat. Ignoring the fresh blood, she moved the bandages back into place and put her shoes back on. She was not going to let the pain stop her. She climbed onto the elliptical machine and pushed through the pain.

4.7… 4.8… 4.9… 5 miles down, she pushed herself further. Her head spun at random intervals since she hadn't eaten that day, but she managed to stay conscious with a few deep, steadying breaths.

On the walk home, Estelle stopped at a CVS pharmacy. After having done research about blister treatment, she grabbed a bag of Epsom salt and stood in the aisle as she read the label.

"Tasteless, colorless, odorless… blah, blah, blah… as a soaking agent… blah, blah, blah… and a laxative? Huh…"

Later, she poured the Epsom salt into her tub and bathed in it, allowing herself enough time to soak her feet thoroughly and calm her racing mind. Afterward, she measured herself again. 109 lbs, and 34-24-34.

Relief swept through her. *Kind of an improvement, but still not good enough…*

She stood in front of her mirror and looked over her body. The bones of her ribcage were slightly visible, and she smiled. *This is definitely an improvement!*

As she lay in bed, she typed into Google search, "iconic gap ads." She scrolled through the result images and noticed a black and white ad with Sofie in it.

This was a campaign they shot last year. How can it already be iconic?

Feeling lost for answers, but determined to prove that she was just as great as Sofie Tsai, she threw her blankets off and stalked over to her closet. She found a similar pair of GAP undies and pulled them on, then removed the rest of her clothing.

In front of her mirror, she snapped a million selfies. She made sure to highlight the makeshift product—her GAP undies while displaying her booty in various attractive poses.

Once she was satisfied, she settled back into bed and opened her Instagram. Immediately checking her notifications, she saw that she had 56 new followers and hundreds of likes and comments. *But still only 21K followers in total…* She speedily edited the picture she'd chosen to use, adding the black and white effect, before posting it with the caption: #gap.

Chapter 3:

The Photographer and the

Top Model

With her eyes closed and her back straight, Estelle tried to meditate. She needed strength, focus, and confidence. She needed this job. She was seated in the waiting room for the GAP casting, along with a crowd of other models—some guys, some girls, and some she couldn't be sure of. She felt overwhelmed when she sat in waiting rooms like this, surrounded by her competition, so she meditated while the rest of them scrolled through Instagram and watched videos on TikTok.

Her eyes flew open when she heard her name called. She stood with a deep breath and walked into the casting room with a wide smile on her face. The models in the foyer were already notified about the casting team—to keep the interviews short and quick—so she already knew who the three people seated behind a table were: the casting director, creative director, and casting assistant.

Estelle handed over her iPad and comp card, then stepped back patiently. They huddled together as they swiped through her portfolio. The casting director looked up at her and smiled as she turned the iPad around.

"Was this a beauty shoot?"

"That—yeah, it was for Smashbox's new foundation called 'Studio skin hydrating foundation.'"

"How recently was that taken?"

Without pause, Estelle rattled off the details of the shoot. "That was taken on a Saturday, June fifth of this year, at Smashbox Studios in Culver City in Los Angeles by Simon Dubois."

She smiled, and the casting trio glanced at one another approvingly. The woman introduced as the creative director spoke up next.

"Are you Korean? Your skin is incredible."

"Oh, thank you. No, my parents were actually born in Cambodia, but we're ethnically Chinese."

"Flawless," she replied, and continued looking over the portfolio before pointing at the screen. "Oh, wow. This one is really interesting. Who shot this?"

Estelle grinned excitedly when she saw which picture it was. "Oh yeah. That was one of the most exciting things I've ever been a part of. It was a collaboration between two pretty big up-and-comers. The designer was Lauren Miller and the photographer was Satoshi Miyazaki. They're so talented." She lifted her hands as she began explaining the shoot in detail.

"They wanted the set design to look like a really elegant, snowy Japanese rooftop garden. We shot it last year on a Tuesday, August 24th on a rooftop in Brooklyn, so it looked like Japan in the foreground and New York in the background."

All three nodded, looking encouraged by her enthusiasm. The casting director spoke again.

"That's beautiful. So, we're just gonna take a few snapshots and your measurements and you'll be all set."

"Great."

The assistant stood and maneuvered Estelle to stand against a white wall to the side, where she took a few snapshots with her iPhone, before measuring her up and calling out the numbers to the casting director.

"33.5-23.5-33.5."

Oh my God, I lost another half inch? Estelle thought excitedly to herself. She watched the casting director cross out her old measurements and write down the new ones. *It's a good sign.* Feeling positive, she picked up her things and thanked them as she left.

***

On a high, Estelle walked along the bustling city streets until she reached Times Square. She felt certain that this time, the casting went well. As she pushed through the crowd, her eyes lifted, and she stopped in her tracks.

What stopped her was the sight of Sofie Tsai on the biggest digital billboard in all of Manhattan. It was an ad for Marc Jacobs' new line of handbags, and Sofie stood looking completely professional with her shoulders hunched, her hair sweeping across her face, and the handbag in her hand.

Estelle gritted her teeth. *I'll get there*, she told herself. *I'll work my ass off until I get there.*

***

The next day Estelle, feeling determined, picked up her walking heels as she headed to her living room. Her bandages were still in place, but bloody puss oozed from the sides as she squeezed her foot into the shoe. She'd developed a certain numbness to the pain, willpower so strong that she no longer winced or limped.

While she practiced, walking up and down, up and down, up and down, she breathed her way through the blood and sweat. When she heard her phone buzzing on the table, she looked over mid-stride. It was Lily. Estelle stopped walking and picked up, catching her breath.

"Hey, Lily."

"You okay?"

"Yeah, no. I'm fine. I was just—I was just working on my walk."

"Ah, always good to hear. I was just calling to say congratulations…"

"What?"

"You booked the GAP shoot." Estelle closed her eyes, absolutely relieved. "They loved you."

"God, I needed this. I'm so broke."

"They said your measurements were actually smaller than what's on your comp card. If so, we need to get those updated."

"That'd be great. Yeah, I've been working really hard, Lil."

"It's paying off."

***

Armed with her tote bag and newly revived confidence, Estelle entered the studio where the GAP shoot was being held. She made her way to a door labeled 'GLAM' and stepped inside. However, instead of making the breezy, cool entrance she'd hoped for, she was taken aback for a moment—because in the very first chair sat Sofie Tsai. She was being done up by a makeup artist, who looked up at Estelle.

"You here for the GAP shoot?"

Estelle struggled to find words, feeling completely thrown by the presence of Sofie. So instead, she tried to focus her mind on the makeup artist who spoke to her. It wasn't hard, since she was a character on her own with a nose ring and immaculate wacky green eye makeup, to match the green tint she had in her blonde hair.

"Uh, yeah, um… Hi, I'm—I'm Estelle."

"Nice to meet you. I'm Byrdie."

Estelle breathed out nervously, relaxing herself, then smiled back at Byrdie. But her calm was short-lived when Sofie turned her chair and looked up at her.

"Hi, I'm Sofie."

"I know…" Estelle replied, completely starstruck. A second makeup artist walked in and grinned at her, taking her arm gently and guiding her to the next chair.

"You can have a seat here, I'm Lindsay, by the way. Any allergies I should be aware of to any specific makeup or latex or anything like that?"

"Not that I'm aware of."

"This shouldn't take long. It's just a simple, clean look for this shoot."

"Great."

As Lindsay prepared her foundation, Estelle glanced to her right and saw Byrdie applying makeup to Sofie's right wrist. She was basically finished so Estelle frowned slightly as she wondered what that was about.

"And you're all done!" Byrdie set her brush down and wiped her hands clean. "I'm gonna run to Crafty. Anyone need anything?"

An array of replies came from the ladies.

"No thanks!"

"I'm good."

While Lindsay began applying makeup to her face, Estelle's eyes peered at Sofie who sat staring down at her phone. She anxiously decided to open conversation and babbled as she tried to think of what to say.

"So, um, oh, you're with Wilhelmina, right?"

Sofie looked up at Estelle's reflection in the mirror and smiled warmly.

"In New York. They're my mother agency. You?"

"Oh, I'm with Ford. I'm also a big fan of yours, by the way… Just saying."

"Oh, really? That's so sweet. Thanks."

Sofie's voice was small but confident. Being only 18 she had the body and traits of a young girl, while her success and years of experience gave her a self-assured personality. Estelle tried to keep still for Lindsay but was enjoying her encounter too much to end the conversation there.

"Yeah, I'm amazed by how long you've already been modeling for. I read you were discovered vacationing in Paris with your family when you were 14?"

"Yeah, and four years later… here we are. It's been… a journey." Sofie reflected.

"Were your parents not suspicious of the scout?"

"They thought it was a kidnapping scam. We didn't even know what modeling was. They wanted me to be a doctor or a lawyer or something." Estelle nodded knowingly, having expected, or hoped, that Sofie's Asian family would be similar to hers. "The first six months were really tough. I went to so many castings and didn't book a single major gig…"

A tough first six months… Estelle thought bitterly. *How about a tough first four years?* No matter what it was, Sofie seemed to have done it better, or gotten it easier. She continued with her story.

"Yeah, but since then I've been on Vogue covers and Times Square billboards, but for my parents, nothing compared to reading about me in the Chinese newspaper for the first time. To them, that was *the* thing. That's what made them go, 'Oh, she's really a model. This can be a real career!'"

Estelle frowned and repeated Sofie's words, remembering what her and Sam had spoken about. "The Chinese newspaper..."

"Yeah, are your parents like that?"

"Yeah, no, I—kind of, I guess."

"How long have you been doing this?"

"I started when I was 16."

"Oh, nice. How'd you end up at Ford?"

"I sent a bunch of photos to different agencies and eventually Ford signed me."

"Oh, so it wasn't like you were just hanging out at a mall and a scout approached you?"

Suddenly feeling inferior, Estelle cleared her throat and shifted in her seat. "Uh, no, it wasn't like—sorry, have you ever worked with Frankie D. before? I'm nervous but excited."

A swift change in topic had Estelle thinking the conversation was saved.

"I have... A few times actually."

Perhaps not. Sofie's answer felt haughty to Estelle, or was she only imagining it out of jealousy? As she tried to hide her embarrassment, Frankie D. walked into the room. Estelle recognized him immediately—he was hard to forget, but not in a good way—he was in his fifties and balding with arms covered in tattoos and he wore signature black-framed glasses. He stopped behind her and put his hand on her shoulder, squeezing it lightly as he introduced himself.

"You Estelle? Frankie D. Looking forward to working with you."

"Me too."

Estelle smiled, feeling even more giddy about the people she was meeting. This was a major job to her, and she could feel the pressure before the cameras were even on her. Frankie D. then turned to Sofie.

"And you… We're ready for you."

Sofie stood and playfully pushed his shoulder. "Pshh, 'and you…' Did you watch that show I told you about yet?"

"That Japanese reality show about seemingly nothing but is oddly addictive anyway?"

"Yeah, you did. Don't act like you didn't watch it."

"I will never admit to watching that."

She joked around with Frankie D. as if they'd been friends for years. The pair headed off to the set while Estelle watched, realizing the rapport between them. She swallowed deeply and couldn't help but think to herself, *that should be me…*

With her makeup finished, Estelle stood next to a table covered with drinks and snacks in the studio. She was sipping black coffee as she watched Sofie do pose after pose, working the camera like the pro she was. Frankie D. encouraged her with every flash of the camera and eventually stood back, nodding his head.

"That's amazing, Sof. I think we got it." He turned to the group of GAP clients who watched from a separate monitor off to the side of the studio. "You guys happy with those?"

They looked up and nodded in agreement. "She looks gorgeous."

"We might just be wrapping up early today folks. Thanks, Sof…" He turned to the shoot stylist, Kelly, standing next to him. "Alright Kels, let's get her into her next outfit. We'll take five. Is Estelle ready to go?"

Kelly nodded at him, before Sofie approached her and said, "I'm gonna grab a coffee. Be right over." She walked to the Crafty table, and after pouring a coffee began sifting through the candy bowl. "Aha! Last one!"

Estelle watched quietly while Frankie D. strolled up as well, and put his hand on Sofie's back.

"What is that? Snickers?"

"Only the best candy ever."

"No way. Milky Way, all the way."

"It's the crunch from the peanuts that make all the difference." Sofie shrugged.

"Yeah, but you know I can't have peanuts."

She frowned. "Why not? Wait, are you allergic?"

"I told you that one night we went out karaoke-ing." Frankie D. told her in a low, comfortable voice. Sofie's face showed confusion.

"Oh yeah! No, I barely remember anything from that night…" She looked embarrassed for a moment, trying to recall when he'd told her about his peanut allergy.

She couldn't remember that night, two years ago, when she went out with him and a few other models and crew members after a shoot. When she belted out the English version of "So Hot" by the Wonder Girls in front of a room full of strangers. When Frankie D. invited her back to his hotel suite because the karaoke club was closing, and they had a few drinks together in the living room…

She shook her head. "Which was kinda weird, 'cause I don't remember even drinking that much, but the next morning I was still super hungover… Anyway, sucky for you then. I love nuts."

There was a brief moment of silence as she reflected back, but she quickly shrugged it off with a nervous smile before tearing open the wrapper of her Snickers bar with her teeth. Frankie D. moved closer to her, trying to keep their conversation private.

"Oh yeah? What about that D? You love that D as well?"

Sofie stepped back, laughing shyly and looking unsure. "Frankie…"

"I'm just talking about vitamin D. What were you thinking?" She merely nodded skeptically, and he carried on. "When was the last time you had a good dose of that vitamin D, huh?"

She awkwardly laughed, writing his words off as a joke, while he started laughing too. They realized Estelle was still standing at the other end of the table, uncomfortably pretending she didn't overhear everything they'd just said. Frankie D. cleared his throat and walked her way.

"Yeah, so, you ready to do this?"

"Uh, oh, uh, yeah."

Estelle shook herself awake again and walked over to the set. She stepped up onto the white cyclorama while Frankie D.'s assistant handed him his camera.

"Alright, Estelle. Show me what you got."

She stood nervously, unsure of what to do. She tried to give him a few different poses, but he immediately commented, "Vary it up a little. Let your arms down."

Her poses looked stiff. From behind his camera, Frankie D. spoke to her. "Loosen up. You can smile.

Be happy. This is GAP. It's all about being youthful and vibrant. Let's see that."

Sofie looked on from the wardrobe corner, where she was being fitted into her next outfit, while Estelle tried, but failed to look natural. She looked nervously around the studio, noticing every face in the room staring at her, waiting for her to display magic in front of the lens. Frankie D. became impatient.

"Hey, you alive? You're a fashion model. Not a mannequin, right? Pose. Show some life. Those clothes are wearing you right now. Come on. Let's go. Models are supposed to be graceful. You're not an Instagram model are you?"

Estelle froze up completely. *No… I am not an Instagram model!* She thought desperately, not able to speak up and tell him so out of sheer anxiety. While she stood as still as a statue, he continued snapping until he realized that she wasn't going to move. He lowered his camera.

"What's going on?"

"I'm sorry."

The creative director who stood to the side of Frankie D. leaned forward and asked her, "You okay?"

Estelle shook her head, trying to snap out of it. "Yeah, sorry. Can I just get a second?"

Frankie D. sighed, unimpressed with her, while she rushed off to the restroom. Even from behind the shut door, she could hear him speaking to the clients.

"Where did you find her? She's lifeless. It shouldn't be that difficult to get something out of a model. Is Sofie ready in her next outfit? We'll have to come back to Estelle. I guess we work around her time…"

Her heart raced as she felt the pressure to perform. She swore she could feel the opportunity slipping away from her as she hyperventilated and tried to calm herself down. She looked ahead of her but her vision narrowed as blackness started to consume her view, and a panic attack set in.

***

Later on, after the shoot had wrapped, Estelle slowly packed her things as Sofie picked up her bag and headed for the door, saying her goodbyes.

"Great working with you guys. I'm sure I'll see you all again."

The makeup ladies replied in unison, "Bye! Pleasure, take care."

Sofie looked at Estelle and spoke kindly, "Hey, you were great today. It was really nice meeting you. Take care."

Estelle flashed her a half-smile, feeling disappointed about the day. "Thanks… Nice meeting you, too."

She felt like she embarrassed herself in front of Sofie, as well as other important people, like Frankie D. Even though she did end up back in front of the camera, calmer and looser, she'd already lost their respect. She wasn't sure how to feel about it, but what she did feel was anger. Towards herself, for screwing up. Towards the camera, for giving her stage fright. And towards Sofie, for always having her shit together. For always being so perfect, all the time. *How does she do it?*

Frankie D. walked up and frowned at Sofie. "You were just gonna leave and not say goodbye?"

"We need to get together and talk about that show you won't admit to watching."

"Oh, we'll definitely get together, but not to talk about that… Bye!" He nodded at her and turned to the makeup girls. "I'm heading out. Great work you two."

"Thanks for having us!"

"See you on the next one!"

He held the door open for them as they wheeled their carts out, before looking at Estelle and nodding curtly. "Estelle, it was nice meeting you today. Have a good night."

"Thanks, it was nice meeting you too," she said, but felt she needed to say something else to explain her weak performance that day. She didn't want him to leave with such a negative first impression of her, so she hastily added, "About earlier, I don't know what—that's never happened to me before. I'm better than that."

He watched her for a moment, then looked around him, making sure everyone else had left before he stepped inside and let the door close behind him, leaving just the two of them alone. He moved towards her and gave her a long, serious stare. "Look, the fashion industry is cutthroat. If you're not able to perform and look the part in a moment's notice, unfortunately, it's onto the next girl. Beauty's extremely common and not difficult to find in New York."

Nodding, Estelle agreed sadly. She knew this. She'd come here today, feeling confident and ready to prove that she could be the next big thing. The next top model. But clearly, other aspects of the day had her overwhelmed before she even stood in front of the camera. She felt like a failure, and his words were confirming just that.

"You know how many calls I get every day from agents and managers of some of the most beautiful girls in the world who say they wanna meet and work with me? More than I can count. I mean look, I think you have a great face, but just being young and cute doesn't separate you from all of the other girls who're trying to do this."

She processed his words, wondering what exactly he meant. Who knew? The modeling industry is about more than just looks? She frowned before asking, "So, is it just about having that 'it' factor then?"

He shook his head. "There's no such thing as an 'it' factor. You think a Wilhelmina model scout knows for certain that the 13-year-old girl they discovered at an Orange Julius in the mall is gonna turn out to be the next Giselle?"

Estelle's eyes were wide as she shook her head, like a child in class, responding with an answer the teacher was already implying quite obviously.

"Of course not. The industry's constantly changing, looking for something new, something different… avant-garde… There's only one thing that separates the top girls from the rest… and that thing is willingness. You have to ask yourself, 'am I willing to do or change to whatever the industry wants me to be?' If a designer told you that you needed to get down to 105 and be 31-21-31 in a month, are you just gonna say no and most likely burn that bridge forever?"

Hell no, Estelle thought.

"Or are you gonna suck it up, bust your ass, and make it happen?

Hell yes. I can do it. 105 and 31-21-31? Easy.

"I mean, what if I asked you to do that? 'Cause the reality is that the top models are the top models because they're willing to do what the other girls won't. They know that in order to achieve greatness, certain sacrifices have to be made. Like, not going out for pizza with your boyfriend on Friday nights 'cause you gotta make sure you fit into that couture dress in the next Balenciaga show three months from now."

She processed what he was telling her while she watched him intently, fascinated by his knowledge and opinions. The mention of pizza and a boyfriend wasn't lost on her either—was that not her Friday nights at Tomato Basil? While she believed that she was willing to do what the other girls wouldn't, she figured she could make a few more sacrifices.

Frankie D. was not finished. He shrugged his shoulders exasperatedly and looked around the room as he thought out his next point. "I mean, look at plus-sized girls. Are they really models? Anyone can sit around on the couch, chompin' on a bucket of fried chicken while watching Real Housewives all day. That sounds awesome, right? I'd love to do that. But how much work does that require? What sacrifices are being made? They aren't willing to put in the work in the gym to improve themselves, 'cause they'd rather gorge on that last glazed doughnut from the dozen. Are we supposed to be rewarding this type of behavior?"

He was laying his opinions on her as if he'd just been waiting for the chance to get them off his chest. His self-assured way of expressing his beliefs on the matter was hypnotic to listen to. Estelle shook her head, in full agreement with him.

"Society seems to be trying to glorify an obese lifestyle as some kinda 'beautiful' thing, but in reality, nobody actually aspires to be fat, do they?" Estelle shook her head quickly, as if he needed the answer from her. "People admire top fashion models and look to them as something to aspire to because those girls watch what they eat and bust their asses in the gym, day after day, to look the way they do. The whole "body positivity" movement… That's just a bullshit way to make overweight girls feel better about themselves 'cause they aren't willing to put in the work and sacrifices it takes to lose weight and be healthy. I mean… You're with Ford, right?"

She was taken aback. *Wow, he knows the agency I'm with?*

"You think a Ford model scout would ever approach a two-hundred pound, 14-year-old girl eating a giant 'Cinna-bun' from Cinnabon at an airport food court? Of course not. Because that's neither healthy or attractive, is it?"

Estelle shook her head vigorously. *Right… He is so right.*

"It's not the 'tolerant' thing to say out in the open, but that's the truth… And I'm betting that scout didn't tell you or your family any of this when they discovered you, did they?"

She thought about her answer. The truth was that she'd been fighting for this since she was 16. She fought for an agent to give her a chance, and she was still fighting her father about her path in life in regards to her chosen career. She'd had to make her own plan to end up where she was. But, that didn't sound very flattering now did it? She swallowed before answering, "Oh, uh, well, my family actually thought it was a kidnapping scam at first..." She scrambled for words, ending up using Sofie's instead. "We were waiting for a flight when the scout approached us. We were vacationing in... Paris."

He nodded. "So, they didn't know anything about the fashion industry. Are they supportive though?"

Estelle shrugged, pretending it didn't matter to her. "My dad wants me to study game theory in economics. My dream is to be on the cover of Vogue. So... basically, the same thing." She laughed nervously. However, her true feelings shone through. "But maybe one day when he sees that cover... he'll actually be proud of me. I don't know…"

Frankie D. didn't say anything for a long moment, taking in her words and formulating his own opinion of her and her hopes for a brighter future. "Well, we all have dreams, don't we? Anyway, if you were worried about today, don't be. Pictures turned out great. Clients were happy. That's all that matters, alright? Alright, I gotta go now. You take care of yourself."

As he left, Estelle put on a half-smile. Even after a long, invaluable chat with a famous photographer, she didn't feel encouraged. She only felt like she had so much more to work on.

Chapter 4:

Lipstick Stains

Feeling equally disappointed and encouraged by the GAP shoot, Estelle met with Lily at the offices of Ford Models. They sat adjacent to each other on couches in a quiet corner with coffee, tea, and pastries arranged on the small table between them. Lily smiled widely as she asked, "So, how'd the GAP shoot go?"

Estelle merely shrugged unexcitedly. "Ehhh, Frankie D. said they were happy about the way everything turned out at the end, so that's all that matters I guess."

"I haven't heard any complaints, so…"

"I've been working on my poses like crazy since then, though. I did 20 different looks the other day at home by myself. Really working on being more like how I should've posed during the shoot…"

Estelle was sitting with her leg tucked under her, so she leaned forward to retrieve her phone from her jeans back pocket. She tapped across the screen before showing Lily the endless pictures she'd taken the previous evening in her apartment. It had taken her a few hours at the least because she included different outfits, underwear, heels, everything she had in order to cover the different kinds of poses she could do. She really pushed herself to get creative and even flipped through her Vogue issues to get some more ideas.

"Jeez, you weren't kidding. You took all these on this phone? How much space do you have?"

"A lot. Yeah, but, uh, about Frankie D., I was wondering if you think you could get me a meeting with him."

Lily lifted her gaze to Estelle's face. "What do you wanna meet him for?"

"I don't want whatever impression he had of me on our shoot to be his last impression of me. I don't know. It might be good to keep that connection open."

Lily nodded with understanding. "I agree. You wanna do a lunch meeting or something?"

"Or just coffee is fine, too."

Lily sat back in her seat and crossed one of her legs over the other. She smiled proudly and gestured towards Estelle. "This is good, Stelle. You're taking steps, trying to grow as a person and grow your network with some important figures in our industry. I'm proud of you. I'll see if he's still in town and try to set something up."

She paused and tilted her head in thought. "Just be careful though. I've dealt with a lot of powerful men in our industry. When you get to the meeting, if he tries to change where it takes place, stay there and call me right away. Don't go anywhere we didn't establish beforehand. Promise me. Got it?"

"Got it. Promise."

∗∗∗

Estelle arrived at The Mark Hotel on Madison Avenue at 77th Street where Frankie D. was staying. Lily managed to get her a lunch meeting with him, and as she entered the lobby she looked from side to side, noticing the bar area where they would meet. When she walked up, she recognized his assistant from the GAP shoot and approached her with a smile.

"Hi, I'm Estelle. I think we met on set the other day. Carson, right?"

The young woman nodded enthusiastically and gestured for Estelle to join her at the table. "Hey, yes. We did."

"Is Frankie D. running late?" Estelle asked and looked around the lavish room.

"No, he's up in his suite on a conference call for a shoot he's doing in Paris next week."

"Wow. Paris? Are you going with him?"

"No, he has another assistant who works out of Paris, another one in Milan. Basically, every major fashion capital. We just coordinate with each other wherever he's going."

"Oh, boo. That's no fun."

Carson laughed lightly at that. "I know. He's always busy. I'm sure you're always busy. You should go meet him. He should be done with his call soon."

"He's coming down, isn't he?" Estelle asked, unsure. Carson lifted her shoulders and spoke slowly.

"Well, you see… He doesn't like discussing work stuff in public." Just then, her phone rang and she picked up within a second. "Hey… Yeah. I'm with her now… Okay." She killed the call and smiled at Estelle, gathering her things to head upstairs.

"I think I need to call my agent and let her know—" Estelle reached for her phone but Carson waved the notion off.

"It's just upstairs. We're not going anywhere."

"Yeah, I understand, but I thought we were having lunch here."

"We're gonna order room service."

"That's—I just don't know how comfortable I feel going up to—"

Carson stopped her mid-sentence with a hand on her arm. "It's just a meeting, Estelle."

She stared at Carson innocently, worried but unsure about the extent of the danger in the situation. "And you'll be there?"

"Of course."

"Ummm, okay… As long as—I guess… Okay, then."

"Great, let's go."

They took the elevator up to the top floor, where the Penthouse Suite was located. When they entered Estelle took a moment to take in her surroundings. The suite was bigger than most two-bedroom apartments in the city, and it was furnished with top-of-the-range couches, tables, and lounge chairs. Through the vast windows she could see a magnificent view of the surrounding high-rise buildings of Manhattan, and beyond the living room was a terrace that overlooked Central Park. It was so grand, Estelle began to feel the weight of exactly who she was meeting with.

Pulling her gaze away, she saw Frankie D. sitting at the dining table, surrounded by printed photos, various documents, and his laptop along with a few camera accessories. He smiled and waved her over. When she sat down, she noticed a variety of Lancôme lipsticks on the table. Frankie D. pointed at them.

"For my Lancôme shoot next week in Paris, they sent me all the different colors to look at. Which is your favorite?"

Estelle looked them over and pointed at one. "Uhhh… This red one, probably."

He nodded and smiled. "You're not hungry?"

He'd already ordered an assortment of foods—the finger-food kind which they could pick at during their meeting. Estelle hadn't touched any of it since she'd entered. Instead, she sat sipping on her black coffee.

"Trying to be more disciplined with my diet, so I can be a better size for designers."

He nodded, seemingly approving of her discipline. "Did you go to Alessandro's casting?"

"Alessandro?"

"Bianchi. He's been in town looking to cast his next runway collection."

She shook her head in confusion. "My agent didn't tell me he was—"

"Oh, you didn't know he was in town?" He turned to Carson. "Hey, I ordered a new lens from B&H. You finished? Pick that up for me?"

While he spoke to Carson, Estelle was still stuck on his previous topic. "Wait, when is the actual show?"

Carson looked at Estelle, remembering the promise she'd made to be around at all times. This wasn't the first time Frankie D. had used her as a "honeypot," but she felt guilty nonetheless about leaving Estelle alone with him. "Uhhh…"

His glare remained on Carson, waiting for her to leave. When she stayed, frozen in doubt at the table, he widened his eyes at her as if to say, *"Get the fuck out… Now!"* She reddened and quickly stood.

"Oh, uh, yeah. Of course. Alright… I'll be back." She picked up her bag and glanced at Estelle one last time before leaving. But Estelle was distracted, she was still wondering why Lily hadn't sent her to the Bianchi casting. Frankie D. watched Carson leave, then turned his attention back to Estelle.

"The show… I don't remember the exact date. It's sometime this month though. You want a drink?" He stood and moved over to a small bar where he began pouring two drinks.

"I'm okay, thank you."

"You're gonna make me drink alone? Come on. Have at least one drink. It's Johnnie Walker Blue."

When he set the drink down in front of her, she reluctantly nodded and took a small sip while she continued to question Lily. "Why didn't she send me out to that casting? Did she not think I was right for it?"

"Who?"

"My agent. She knows how hard I've been working on my walk and my body."

"Have you…" Frankie D. said slowly as he settled into a lounge chair with his drink, and lifted the corner of his mouth in a cool smile.

Estelle nodded quickly, and pulled out her phone to show him the photos she'd taken. Without much thought, she shifted her chair closer to his and leaned closer towards him. "Can I show you something? Since our shoot, I've been really working on my poses."

"Oh yeah? Alright, lemme see…"

He leaned in closer, looking at the pictures with feigned interest before his eyes darted to her face and he licked his lips.

Estelle was oblivious to his actions as he lifted a hand and touched her cheek, turning her face and planting a kiss on her lips. Startled, she pulled back and quickly stood to her feet. With wide eyes, she stared at him incredulously while he watched her with calm eyes.

"Whoa…"

"You okay? What's wrong?"

"What do you mean—what are you doing?" she stammered.

"We got this entire suite to ourselves." Frankie D. looked completely nonplussed, smiling and waving his hand about the suite. Estelle stood still with an open mouth, unsure of what to say, what to do, or even how to stand. Her arms crossed in front of her chest as she searched for a reason, any reason that would help her say no. Because she knew that she couldn't offend him. If she did that, she didn't know how he'd react—and she didn't want to find out.

"I have a boyfriend."

He shrugged. "Okay? We can still have fun. I'm not looking to date."

"What is this?"

"You wanted to meet. This is how meetings work in our industry."

"What do I look like to you?" Estelle asked, her voice rising with the anger that was warming her cheeks and causing every limb to tense up.

After a brief pause of thought, he leaned backward in his chair and spoke very candidly. "You look like someone who needs help breaking through in the modeling world. Isn't that why you're here?"

Estelle realized her mistake. She'd come to him; she'd asked for this. She felt a sudden shame while Frankie D. carried on talking calmly as if he were giving her advice. "I can be that help. Alessandro and I go way back. I've shot a number of his campaigns. I can get you into his casting."

Her eyes darted to his. She wanted desperately to know how, but she was too afraid to go there. She stood still but vibrated with fear and anger.

"Tell me, do you know how Sofie Tsai landed her first cover of Vogue?" She shook her head. "I was shooting it, and I put in a good word for her. I *could* put in a good word for you, too. I mean, if you want, but why would I *just* do that?"

In a small, trembling voice, she knew what her next question needed to be, in order for her to walk out of the suite with something to show for the day. "What do you want?"

He smirked, knowing he'd already won. He leaned slowly back and jerked his head towards the lipsticks on the table. "You said that red one was your favorite, right? Lipstick stains are always fun…"

His eyes shifted down to his crotch, and her face drained of all color. The voice in her mind that had been quietened until now, boomed through her head. He saw her inner turmoil and continued to speak in a deceivingly reassuring voice.

"Relax… I'm not forcing you to do anything. There's no pressure. If you're willing to hang and have a little fun… Great. If not, you're free to leave whenever you want. Door's over there… But good luck with your career."

Is he threatening me? Estelle let out the breath she'd held deep in her chest, before asking, "You'll get Bianchi to see me for his show? You promise?"

"I've made a lot of girls' careers—Sofie's, Gigi, Bella, Kaia, you name 'em… Your agent will get a call from Alessandro's team saying he wants to see you for his casting."

Amidst her whirlwind of emotion, Estelle frowned. *Is that even true? Would he lie about something like that?* However, whether it was or wasn't true, she had no authority at that moment and was in no position to question it.

In order to build up her career, she'd have to make sacrifices. Not only did she need this casting as if it were the last one on Earth, but she also felt trapped. Because she knew that she was caught at a crossroads—if she said yes, she could advance her career immensely. But if she said no, she might as well kiss her dreams goodbye.

She closed her eyes and nodded slowly, accepting her fate. Frankie D. stood with a creepy smile on his face. He reached for the lipstick she'd chosen and smeared it messily over her lips. After throwing it aside, he sat on the couch and made himself comfortable.

Estelle couldn't get herself to move straight away. She stood, shoulders lifted and arms crossed, trying to find strength. His eyes raked over her body.

"What would you like me to tell Alessandro about how your body looks? You say you've been working hard on it but with everything you're wearing it's really hard for me to judge…"

Her lips started to quiver, and her eyes welled up with tears. Her mascara began to run down her cheeks as she slowly began to undress. Frankie D. unbuckled his belt, unzipped his pants, and pulled himself out, stroking and shifting as he readied himself. She pulled her gaze away, completely repulsed by him and ashamed of herself.

He watched her go through the motions and spoke earnestly. "I honestly believe you should see this as a good thing. You're using the fact that you're a pretty young girl to your advantage. I challenge anyone to find me some female 48-year-old film producer or executive that a no-name 20-year-old boy with big dreams would be able to fuck for a starring role in her production. Cute girls at least have the option to give head to get ahead."

He watched her with an eerily silent, menacing air while Estelle pulled the last of her clothing off. When she was fully naked, she remained standing awkwardly in front of him, desperately trying to retain what little dignity she had left by crossing her arms over her exposed breasts, her hands clinging to each shoulder, and her leg tightly folded across the other.

He watched her standing there, then looked down as if to say, *"What are you waiting for?"* Hot tears streamed down her face as she slowly moved down onto her knees in front of him. He immediately took a hold of her hair and pushed her head into his lap.

Five minutes. Perhaps not even that, and it was over. The most disgusting thing she had ever done, had come and gone already. Her head spun with questions and accusations as she stumbled into the restroom and puked on the floor, missing the toilet bowl. She looked down, and a strong voice in her mind told her: *Don't clean it up. Fuck him.*

She turned to the sink and rinsed out her mouth, cupping the water and splashing her face as trembles refused to let her hands keep steady. She looked into the mirror, and feeling utterly disgusted with herself, grabbed a hand towel and frantically wiped the red lipstick from her lips, struggling to get it all off. There were still faint red smudges around her lips, and a smear up her right cheek that refused to be erased, but she didn't care. She needed to get out of there, immediately.

When she stepped out of the restroom, she saw Frankie D. at the table, casually eating his lunch as if nothing had just happened. She grabbed her purse and turned to leave, before hearing his voice directed at her.

"I'm glad we had this meeting. You can expect a call."

Without so much as a glance, she left the suite.

Chapter 5:

Culture Clash and Filial

Piety

Estelle lit up a cigarette and inhaled deeply. Her hands shook each time she raised it to her lips. The smoke plumed around her as she sat on her balcony, shivering from the cold, which she barely noticed. Her dead eyes stared at the floor; there was nothing going through her mind. That loud voice she'd heard before was once again shoved down into the darkest corner of her mind, where it sat screaming inaudibly.

Her phone vibrated next to her, making her jump in fright. She eyed the screen, seeing the text notification and reached out for it.

> Sam: Haven't heard from you all day. Everything okay?

Without a thought, she locked her phone and set it back down.

***

While on her shift at Tomato Basil, Estelle kept herself distracted and busy with her work. She set plates down for a group of two as Sam approached her, asking her quietly, "I feel like you're avoiding me. Are you still mad about that Asian parent joke?"

She looked at him blankly, before turning away and grabbing plates from a nearby empty table. As she deposited them in the kitchen, she felt her phone buzz and stepped into the backroom to answer it.

"Hey, Lily. What's up?"

"Alessandro Bianchi wants to meet you for his new runway collection."

"When? Now? I'm at work. I'm off in a few hours. I can head straight there after."

"It's either now or I have to tell them you can't make it."

She only needed a second to think about what to do. "…I'll be there."

Putting the phone down, she thought for a moment. *Okay, so I got the casting. This is great news.* But the reason she got it flashed through her mind, and she had to take a few calming breaths before walking out and approaching her manager.

"Hey, Jimmy."

He'd just finished pushing the kitchen staff for faster orders. The restaurant was packed, and Estelle wondered how she was going to get this right. He wasn't an unreasonable man, but he was running a popular restaurant after all. He turned to her and answered quickly.

"What's up, Stelle?"

"So, my agent just told me about a casting for a really big designer…"

"Okay?"

"So, I was wondering if it'd be okay for me to go to that casting right now and come back afterwards."

"You serious? We're slammed. I mean, I know this is just a part-time job for you, but—"

"I promise I won't be long." She put up her hands in a show of faith, cutting him off, but he shook his head.

"I need you here."

Sam walked into the kitchen and dropped a few dirty dishes onto the counter, then looked over at Estelle and Jimmy curiously. Estelle had her head in her hand before shrugging hopelessly.

"Okay, then… I guess I have to quit. I need to make it to this casting."

Jimmy stood still with his face creased in disbelief. "You're gonna quit this job for a potential job you might not get?"

"You've no idea what I had to do to get this opportunity. I don't know if I'll get another chance. I have to take it." What she'd had to do was a sacrifice that couldn't be left without reaping the outcome. Jimmy sighed and shook his head, giving up.

"Alright, good luck with everything, girl. Get outta here."

"Thank you for everything."

She nodded with a small smile before heading across the kitchen and removing her apron. Sam, still watching, moved closer as she was heading out.

"Seriously, what's going on?"

Estelle looked his way and stopped. She couldn't do this. She couldn't lie to Sam about what she'd done, and she couldn't explain herself to him all the time. She needed to focus on her career if she was ever going to make it. "I don't wanna be with you anymore," she said straight to his face.

His mouth dropped open; had he heard her correctly? Flabbergasted, he racked his brain for what might have changed things, but no, as far as he could remember, everything had been perfect until now. This sudden rift between them had come out of nowhere and he couldn't even comprehend what had pushed her so far away from him. He stopped her with a gentle hand on her shoulder.

"Hey, wait. Stelle—"

She spun around and cut him off. "I have goals and ambitions and things I needa do in order to achieve my dreams. You've been here for two years, and you're not even trying to do anything with your life. I spend all day watching what I eat and working my ass off in the gym. You watch people playing video games on YouTube while eating pizza and breadsticks in front of me. Don't you see? I can't just be a product of my environment. I want more for you than you want for yourself. I'm never gonna move up in life with you because people only improve when they surround themselves with others who're self-motivated, driven, and better than they are… I'm sorry."

He watched her leave while the hurt he felt glistened in his eyes.

***

Estelle made it to the casting, out of breath but ready to impress. She stood in front of Alessandro Bianchi as he sat with his team. He was middle-aged with his hair swept over and immaculately groomed.

Standing tall and stoic, she had her chin up and her shoulders back. The group whispered as they swiped through her portfolio, glancing up at her every now and then. She took their short nods and quick glances as good signs, and tried to breathe more easily.

***

Later that evening Estelle sat with her family while they ate dinner at her parents' house. Her younger sister, Christian, joined this time. She was 19 and had come by after finishing school for the day. While their father read the Chinese newspaper, Estelle picked at her food and Christian racked up conversation.

"Anything new with life or is it still just modeling stuff?"

"I just did a GAP shoot. It was shot by Frankie D. He's a major photographer in the industry."

Christian nodded, the look on her face saying, *So still just modeling stuff then…* "Is it like a commercial or something?"

"No, it's an e-com job."

Richard looked up from his paper excitedly. "Economic?"

"No, 'e-com,' not 'econ.' E-commerce. How do you model economics?"

"I don't know. Ask your sister? That's her major."

Her family laughed at that. She tried to explain it, wanting her family to understand and be invested in her passions. "You know what you see online? The clothes the models are wearing. That's e-commerce stuff."

"I don't online buy clothes," her father said frankly.

Estelle gave up trying, instead looking at her untouched food while she added, "Well, that's that. I think I might also be featured in some of their print ads too."

"How much did it pay?"

She sighed, dropping her chopsticks onto her plate. "Knew it... Not saying money isn't great. It's important, but that job was more than just a paycheck. It's a big step forward in my career. I got to work with one of the most highly renowned photographers in the world. Biggest one I've ever worked with actually."

"Your sister is going to get paid to be intern for Merrill Lynch next summer."

"Oh... Congratulations..."

Estelle felt disregarded. Completely ignored and misunderstood. Was it too much to ask for her family's support? Did she always need to be compared against not only her younger sister but the entirety of the Chinese race, too? Christian wasn't the type to gloat, but she smiled at her father's approval.

"Thanks. Apparently, my future supervisor handles P. Diddy's money."

Estelle eyed her father as she answered. "Wow, are you excited or is he more excited about it than you?"

"Of course she ex-sigh-ding. It's uh-Merrill Lynch. Come on." Richard lifted his hands in exasperation.

May, sensing tensions rising between her daughters and husband, quickly scooped some more food onto Christian's plate, then pointed at her hair. *"After we finish eating, can you help me dye my hair?"*

"Okay, okay…" Christian nodded at her docile mom. But Richard wasn't finished.

"She go to Columbia with full scholarship and now Merrill Lynch next summer. I don't have to give her a penny. Your younger sister is on a good path. We can tell our friends about her because what she is doing is respeck-uh-table. I don't have to worry 'bout her."

"Okay? That's great." Estelle shrugged, unsure about how it related to her aspiring career or to the modeling industry and what she needed to do to become a top model.

"You just asked me for money last month."

"I'm gonna pay you back after I get this check from my GAP job. The photoshoot I did before GAP was an editorial, so it wasn't paid, and I needed a new outfit for a certain casting because I didn't have the right clothes for it."

"Wait, you needed to borrow money… to buy different clothes… for a casting?" Christian asked, her eyebrow raised.

"You can't just go in with the usual jeans and T-shirt for certain designer castings."

Richard scoffed. "Re-dick-a-lus. Tell you what, you don't need to pay me back. I will even give you more money if you quit the modeling and go study game theory… Think about it."

Estelle kept quiet, continuing to pick at her food, while her mother leaned closer to her. *How come I never see you eating? You're so skinny.*

"You don't understand," Estelle replied in Mandarin, out of respect for her mother, but reverted to English so she could make her point clear. "I need to lose inches. Right now, I'm not the perfect size, and if I'm not the perfect size, clients are just gonna find someone else who is, and I can't have that."

"What's the perfect size? Skeletal?" Christian asked, her sarcasm bordering on the edge of mockery. Estelle shook her head, unable to believe her own sister wouldn't back her up.

"I don't know why I thought you'd be more supportive…"

"I'm not *un*-supportive…"

Estelle sighed. "You know what? Here's what I think: I think if girls aren't willing to put in the work and sacrifices then they should just quit. That's my opinion. It'll just make it easier for me to book jobs. Or go plus-sized. Then you can just eat fried chicken all day."

Christian wondered if her sister had always been this way. Surely, she could remember a time when Estelle hadn't been so… judgmental? She discarded the thought and softened, realizing that her sister was in fact trying really hard to make it in her industry. "There are more things to life than just modeling, you know? How's Sam?"

"Yeah, he have new job yet or still working at the restaurant with you?" Richard added, and Estelle averted her gaze in annoyance. "I'm worried, can he take care of you? He is still working there means he doesn't have money."

Shaking her head, Estelle kept her mouth shut. She knew he would bring that up.

"Love is also important, Dad," Christian added, trying to back her sister up before a fight ensued.

But Estelle wasn't having it and scoffed at Christian. "Love? Really? He once told me, 'Afsur twensie years of marriage? What'sa love? Your mom only marry me to escape Pol Pot and Cambodia.'"

"She didn't mean that…" Christian frowned and turned to their mom, asking in Mandarin, *Is that true?*

May wasn't going to disagree with her husband. Instead, she tried to explain their circumstances to the girls. *"Do you know how bad it was under Pot? Four years in a labor camp? We came to America because we wanted to give you two better opportunities for your future..."*

Christian took her words in, not sure what to make of it. Estelle merely shrugged. *Told you so.*

"Well, do you love Sam?"

She didn't answer. Her sister and her father shared a look, they had their answer. Meanwhile, May gave Christian another reminder by pointing to her hair again.

"You finished yet? It's getting late."

Chapter 6:

#thinsperation and the

Next Kate Moss

Estelle struggled to get up the next morning. She still felt tired and had a headache that sent sharp pains jolting to the spot between her eyebrows. Dragging her bandaged feet, she headed to the bathroom and went about her morning routine.

As usual, she stepped on the scale while brushing her teeth: 108 lbs. Her eyes lit up and she spat her toothbrush into the sink.

"Fuck yes."

She quickly grabbed the tape and measured herself: 33-23-33. She'd lost another half-inch all around. Excited, she spat out the rest of the toothpaste.

"Fuck yes!"

She rinsed her mouth out and looked into the mirror, smiling, thinking her day was turning around. Except as she looked up, she noticed multiple zits forming on her cheeks.

"Fuck, shit!"

Once dressed, with white pimple cream caked over the zits on her face and fresh bandages over her blisters, Estelle plopped herself down onto her couch. Grabbing her laptop from the coffee table, she crossed her legs and opened it, checking her email.

There was a new one from Lily, and she immediately clicked on it:

> *…They said he really thinks you have an immaculate face and that they loved you in person. They also think your personality is great... However, they don't think you'll fit in with the other models in their current lineup because of your height. So, unfortunately, they didn't pick you this year. But don't be discour—*

Slamming her laptop closed, Estelle fumed. *After all I did! Everything I sacrificed! It was all for nothing!* She stomped to her bedroom and got into her gym clothes. Working her ass off was going to be her way to expel her frustrations and prove to everybody that she could do it.

At the gym, she sat in the sauna after her workout. She was wrapped in a towel and covered in sweat as she brooded alone in the quiet and stuffy room. The steam filled her lungs, and she took a deep breath to calm her nerves, except it didn't help at all. She let the breath out in a loud, solitary scream from the top of her lungs, that reverberated against the walls, heard by no one except her.

Soon after, her head popped out of the sauna door as she checked her surroundings and walked out, completely—yet falsely—composed. Sauntering over to her locker she dropped her towel and pulled her underwear on. A passer-by glimpsed her bony rib cage and quickly looked away.

Estelle stepped over to a full-length mirror with her phone and admired her figure through another ten selfies. She picked one that showcased her scrawny torso and hollow cheeks, quickly editing out the red zits before posting it to her Instagram page with the caption:

> *For relaxing times, make it sauna-tori-time. #model, #asianmodel #thinsperation #bonespo #glassskin #workout #relax #sauna #sofiacoppola #lostintranslation #tokyo #favoritefilm #love.*

***

Sat down in the consultation room of a well-known cosmetic surgeon, Estelle listened carefully as the smug-looking man showed her sample X-ray photos of a limb lengthening procedure.

"And I would have to break the tibia and fibula in two, so that I can insert a telescoping rod into your cartilage. Over a period of about three months, the rod will slowly pull your bones apart, roughly about a millimeter a day, then as the bones in your legs are stretched apart, your body's natural healing response is to grow new bone, nerves, arteries, and skin to renew the area and basically, fill in the gaps. It's a tricky balance though. Your bones have to be stretched out slowly enough so that new bones continue to grow but also fast enough so that it doesn't heal too quickly because if it heals too quickly—"

"Then the bones won't grow, and it'll all be worthless."

"Exactly... But I've had plenty of success with this type of surgery, so I feel very confident in my ability to perform this procedure. Not even God can do what I do." Estelle raised an eyebrow, not exactly impressed with the smirk on the egotistical surgeon's face, but still very intrigued about the procedure. "This is usually a three-to-five-month process with physical therapy afterwards. But I do have to say you're already pretty tall for a woman, so I don't really think you need this."

Not tall enough… she thought and disregarded his advice. "How much does it cost?"

***

That evening Estelle visited her sister on the Columbia University campus. They sat in the cafeteria and Christian pigged out on pasta while Estelle sipped her black coffee. With a full mouth, Christian eyed Estelle's cheeks and said, "Your face…"

"I know."

"You're flaring—"

"I know." Estelle cut her off in frustration.

"You've lost more weight…"

"I know!" she answered excitedly.

Her sister looked up with an expression that said, *that's not a good thing…* But Christian quickly brushed it off and asked, "Everything else going okay? When can we see those GAP pictures?"

"I don't know. Whenever they post them online? Not really thinking about that anymore. Kinda just trying to focus on what I needa do next."

"Oh, good. You have another job booked?"

"I needa borrow money."

She nodded, thinking perhaps Estelle needed groceries. "How much?"

"25 thousand."

Quickly swallowing her food, Christian's eyebrows furrowed deeply. "What? Why?"

"I'm not tall enough. I'm tired of not being considered for jobs or not getting them because I'm shorter than other girls."

"Okay? But why do you need 25 *thousand* dollars?"

"For limb lengthening surgery. Alessandro Bianchi thinks I'm great, but I'm just too short."

"So what? Who is that?"

"Are you kidding? He's only one of the biggest couture fashion designers in the world. What he thinks about me is important."

"I mean, I—I don't even know what to say…"

Estelle sat without moving, without showing any emotion. "Christian, can I borrow the money or not?"

"You think I even have 25 thousand dollars to lend you?"

Estelle shrugged, acting like it was a no-brainer. "Can't you take out a student loan or something? I'll pay you back once I book a few more jobs—and don't tell the parents—25 thousand is a small price to pay for a career that's potentially going to bring in millions."

"I'm not taking out a student loan and going into debt just so you can use it on a surgery you don't even need."

"Did you not hear what I said? I'm at a disadvantage for jobs."

Christian stared at Estelle. *She's delusional.* Everything she was saying was pure insanity. She tried to think of a way to relate to her sister's thought process, to get her to see some resemblance of logic. "You think Kate Moss, Devon Aoki, or Jenny Shimizu ever considered doing something like this? They made it because of everything else they are."

"Well, they're still limited to what they can do. Plus, Devon Aoki and her brother were born into Benihana money. That's not a fair comparison."

Christian sighed, dropping her fork. *Nothing I say will help.* "You don't need to get every job, every show, every campaign, every whatever else—what does your agency think about this? Did you discuss this with them?" Estelle glanced away, grinding her teeth in irritation while Christian continued. "Every surgery comes with risks—big or small—something could happen. I'm not gonna encourage this and put you at risk. If you need a loan, you're gonna have to take one out yourself."

"I tried. I didn't get approved 'cause I quit Tomato Basil. Promise me you won't tell the parents. I'm already enough of a disappointment to Ba. I don't needa hear anymore from him again."

Christian's heart sank for her sister, knowing there was nothing else she could do to help her see the light. Estelle was too stubborn and too disgruntled to listen to reason. She would have to find a way to be there for her sister that didn't include pushing her away for life. Because at this point, Estelle seemed to be in a "ride or die" kind of mindset. It was her way, or no way at all. Christian nodded solemnly with a drop of her shoulders and softened her tone.

"Okay, I won't say anything. Promise."

***

Cars honked, pedestrians shouted, and music blared—but Estelle heard nothing as she stood on her balcony, periodically pulling on her cigarette. Her eyes stared out into the distance, searching for answers, pondering her life.

She didn't even startle when her phone rang, she merely realized that it was ringing at some point, and quickly looked at the screen before answering.

"Hey, Lily... Uh, yeah. Yeah, I'll—I can be there in a bit. Yeah, do I have to be worried? Okay... Okay... Good... See you soon. Okay, bye."

She hurried inside and put on some makeup—covering her acne, before rushing out the door and into the subway.

Once she was sitting next to Lily in the lounge area of Ford Models, Estelle felt dread in her stomach.

"You're not dropping me, are you?"

Lily pulled back with a frown. "Why would you think that?"

"I just—I don't know... 'cause I haven't booked many jobs this season?"

"What? No, Stelle, I asked you here 'cause I have some major news I wanted to tell you in person. Just try not to freak out, okay?"

Lily paused, and Estelle became impatient. "What? What is it?"

"Bianchi's people called me back again today... and said he decided you are gonna be in his lineup after all."

She looked at Lily, waiting for the punchline, but it never came. "No... You're kidding. Lil, don't joke. Tell me you're serious."

"I'm serious. Congratulations!"

"Oh, my goodness..." Estelle hugged Lily tightly, making her laugh before pulling back and putting her hand over her mouth. She couldn't believe it. "What made him change his mind?"

> *In Bianchi's atelier, he stood with his team staring at a model board with fingers to their lips. At the top of the board said, "Alessandro Bianchi F/W 2021 Women's Runway," and below there were photos of 50 female models—headshots and full-body shots.*
>
> *They were trying to make a final decision on the casting for the runway show, but Bianchi felt something didn't feel right. Frustrated, he pulled one of the pictures down and flicked it onto the table nearby, where there was a stack of rejected models' photos. He stood back again, frowning at the board as he tried to figure out what was missing, when his assistant approached him with Estelle's printouts that she'd taken from the table of discarded pictures.*
>
> *"What about Estelle Li?"*

Lily leaned towards Estelle and lifted her eyebrows. "And you'll never guess what else he said about you..."

"What?"

Estelle's mouth dropped open. "No, he didn't..."

"Apparently, he did."

Lily smiled and laughed as they hugged excitedly. She was happy that Estelle finally had some good news to bring her spirits and motivation back up. She held her tightly, as if she were trying to pour all her happiness into the embrace. She would never tell her, but she saw her younger self in Estelle. Through all the obstacles, the hills and fucking mountains that grew in her pathway, she pushed through with her fierce determination.

Estelle breathed more easily when they pulled apart and smiled as she considered Bianchi's words: *Heroin chic... The next Kate Moss...*

Chapter 7:

Heroin ~~Chic~~ Addict

In order to get his next collection just right, Bianchi was working closely with his assistants and seamstresses when Estelle entered his atelier. This new collection was inspired by George Tooker's *Bathers*, and he had mannequins scattered around with various dresses on them that all needed to be custom tailored to perfectly fit their respective models' bodies. One, in particular, had a 1950s-style swim cap made up of cherry blossoms.

Estelle stood on a platform as her outfit was being fitted. Bianchi fluttered around her and spoke to the seamstress in his thick Italian accent, jabbing his finger towards the material.

"No, no, no... This... This—this right here needs to come in some more. It shouldn't be so fucking loose. She's not a fucking coat hanger even if she looks like one. Fix it!"

Without so much as a glance towards Estelle's face, he moved on to the next model. Yet, she smiled, flattered by his comment about her being as skinny as a fucking coat hanger. She glanced over and saw Sofie strolling in, looking like the million-dollar supermodel she was. She saw Estelle and grinned.

"Heeeeeey, how are you?"

"Hey, good. Great... You don't remember my name, do you?"

"Sorry... I'm good with faces, just not with names."

"Estelle Li."

"Right, Estelle. How are you? I didn't know you were gonna be in this show."

Estelle's mouth opened slightly, finding Sofie's nonchalant attitude offensive. "Why? Do you think you're the only Asian model in the world or something?"

Sofie's brows furrowed in confusion. "No... I didn't mean that. I just—they must've updated the lineup. Never mind that I said anything—"

Bianchi appeared next to Sofie. "Ah, Sofie..."

A relieved Sofie smiled, "Alessandro..." They greeted each other with kisses on both cheeks, European style.

"Sofie, love. How are you, my dear? Go see Maria. She'll get you into your piece. I'll check up on the fit when you're in it." He leaned into her and whispered. "And guess what..."

"What?"

"You're going to open the show."

Estelle overheard and annoyance built in her chest. Meanwhile, Sofie tried her best to contain her excitement and put a hand to her chest. "Really? Oh, my gosh. I'm so honored."

"You're going to love what I have for you, so go get dressed."

"I'm sure I will."

Estelle rolled her eyes dramatically and mouthed 'bitch' at Sofie as she headed off. Bianchi turned back to look over Estelle. His eyes dropped to the seamstress who was bent down, dabbing a cloth at Estelle's feet. He stepped forward with a frown and spoke to the seamstress.

"What are you doing down there?"

Her voice was small as a mouse, as she tried to explain. "I don't know what..."

There was an odd, maroon-like color blooming all around the designer heels on Estelle's feet. The color palette of Bianchi's collection had no maroon. The heels were supposed to be baby blue. Bianchi looked between Estelle and her feet.

"Are you bleeding?"

Still staring at Sofie who'd walked off, Estelle snapped back to reality. "What? I'm sorry?"

"Your feet. What's happening?" His voice hung in the air as he waited for her reaction.

"What?" She looked down and noticed the blood seeping into the fabric of the heels. Her blisters had opened up when she put the heels on. "Oh, my God... I'm so sorry. No—I'm fine. Oh, my God..."

His eyes drilled into hers. "Those were three-thousand-dollar heels."

"I'm so—"

"You know what?" He stopped her and lifted his hands in the air. "Take care of your feet. I just decided I'm going to make you a special heel for this show. It'll be an extra-long one to make up for you being a midget." She was relieved to hear him let it go so easily, flattered by his special plan for her, then offended by his ultimate insult about her height. "So make sure you can walk in them."

"I will."

"Very good, darling." He nodded quickly, then turned to the seamstress. "Get those cleaned up, so we can make a new heel for her. I don't want to see a spot of red on them either."

"Yes, sir." The young seamstress was flustered from his quick orders and looked up at Estelle. "Can you lift your foot up?"

***

Estelle was once again bathing in Epsom salt. She lifted her legs out of the water and frowned despairingly at the red sores on every corner of her feet. After the bath, she sat down on the toilet, carefully dried her feet, then reapplied fresh bandages to the blisters. In the living room, she stuffed thick wads of tissue paper into her practice heels before slipping them on. She needed to practice walking in higher heels for the show, so she improvised.

She strode up and down her living room, putting as much concentration into her catwalk as she possibly could, desperate to get it just right. In the mirror, she saw herself panting with exertion and dipped her eyes to her body. Her figure looked skeletal. But she smiled, proud of the hard work she'd done.

With a swift turn, she started another lap, staring straight ahead with her shoulders back, chin up, completely stoic as she walked like a seasoned professional. Concentrating hard, she didn't notice when a drop of perspiration broke free from her hairline, ran down her forehead… past her eyebrow… and right into her eye. The salt from her sweat burned her pupils and she squeezed her eyes shut, cringing at the pain.

As her hand flew up to wipe her eye, her foot wobbled in the ridiculously high heels and she stumbled across the living room. As she reached for the couch to steady herself, her right ankle rolled, snapping inward. A loud crack sounded through the room, filling her soul with dread.

Her bloodshot eyes shot open, and she screamed in pain. As she clutched her ankle, realization dawned. She shook her head as tears welled in her eyes. "Oh, no! No, no, no, no, no…" She immediately knew she was fucked.

***

The following morning, Estelle woke up wincing in pain. Looking down, she saw that her blistered feet had bloodied her white sheets, and the bandages that had come off during the night were scattered throughout her bed. Her right ankle was swollen to the size of a tennis ball.

She groaned as she slowly tried to get out of bed without putting any weight on her right foot. However, her attempts were in vain as the blisters on her left foot seared with pain anyway, the thin skin of the pustules popped open and left a trail of blood in her wake. In her bathroom she glanced at herself in the mirror, noticing a few more zits that had materialized overnight.

Trying hard not to freak out, she lowered herself onto the toilet and peed. Even that was painful. Her entire body was angry, lashing back at her for the pain she was putting it through. She wasn't eating, she wasn't resting, and she was stressed the hell out.

She lifted her right ankle to take a look, and her spirits dipped again when she saw the odd discoloration—an ugly mixture of green, yellow and purple. Lowering her foot carefully, she reached for her flushable wipes and cleaned the blisters. Her eyes watered as she sighed and shook her head. *I need help…*

She called her sister, who answered the phone without greeting. "I'm not taking out a student loan…"

***

Christian let herself into Estelle's apartment with her spare key. The place was eerily quiet, and she walked through to the bedroom. What she saw nearly broke her heart. Estelle's body lay across her bed, bony and white. She looked like a rotting corpse. Estelle heard her enter and lifted her head slowly to look at her.

"God, Stelle. You look like a heroin addict…"

Shaking her head, Christian stepped closer and inspected her swollen ankle, while Estelle winced in pain.

***

The two sisters listened to Dr. Madeleine while she explained Estelle's X-ray results. Estelle lay on a bed with her foot propped up and Christian stood next to her with her arms crossed in a serious manner.

"Fortunately, the bone isn't broken or fractured. The swelling always looks worse than it is. That'll, of course, reduce over time."

"How long before I can walk again?"

"I'd say about a month."

"A month? But the show is in two weeks."

Christian sighed. "Stelle... you can't even stand."

The doctor looked between the two of them. "What show?"

"I'm a fashion model. I'm supposed to walk the runway for Alessandro Bianchi's upcoming collection."

"I'm sorry, but you just need to rest and let it heal. I strongly advise against putting any weight on your foot right now. And as for these blisters, an over-the-counter antibiotic ointment will do."

***

Back at Estelle's apartment, Christian helped her onto the couch with a small bag of medication and a bottle of water from the nearby CVS pharmacy. Her ankle was wrapped up in a medical bandage.

"You need anything else? If not, I have to go study."

"Yeah," Estelle nodded and pointed towards her bedroom door. "Can you go to my closet and grab my heels for me?"

Christian frowned deeply at her. "Why?"

"The show's in two weeks. I need to practice walking in higher heels."

"Are you fucking kidding?" Christian stared at her in utter disbelief, before shaking her head and muttering to herself, "I can't believe you're the older sibling." Then she reached for the medicine and dropped it onto Estelle's stomach. "The doctor said not to put any weight on your foot."

Estelle gestured down to her foot. "It's tightly wrapped. Look."

"What if you make it worse? What if you twist your other ankle?"

"I'll tape the other ankle for support when I practice. Can you just get them for me?"

"No! I have an exam I needa study for. If you want me to bring you food or something—*then* call me."

"I don't need food. I needa be able to walk in this upcoming show."

Christian scoffed. "Unbelievable."

"What?"

Her patience had run out. It was one thing to help a sister in need, but another if she was going to lie there and make unreasonable demands. Christian didn't know what to do anymore. She'd been understanding until now; she'd even put her own hard work and priorities aside for Estelle, but it was starting to feel like a lost cause. If Estelle wanted to go down this road of self-sabotage, there was not much more she could do to stop her. She put her fingers onto the bridge of her nose to control her frustration. "You are so selfish and ungrateful, you know that? Everything's always about you."

Estelle was quiet for a second, thinking over her sister's words, before looking away. "Don't you have to go study?"

Christian rolled her eyes and turned to leave, shutting the door behind her without looking back.

Chapter 8:

Tongue

Later in the evening, Estelle was on the couch, icing her ankle when there was a knock on her door. She looked up and called out, "It's open!"

Lily entered tentatively, holding a stack of magazines and peering through the doorway. She saw Estelle and greeted her gently. "Hey... How ya feelin'?"

"Just... terrific." Estelle answered, trying her best to look undeterred. Lily sat down on the couch next to her.

"How bad is it?"

"Bad? It feels great, Lil." She chuckled lightly, lifting her shoulders as if it was nothing serious.

Lily took a closer look at Estelle's sprained ankle with narrowed eyes. "Glad you still have a sense of humor. I didn't think it would look this bad... Here, brought you these—" With a smile Lily handed Estelle a variety of new fashion magazines, including Vogue, Numéro, I-D, Elle, Highsnobiety, and the like. "Hopefully these'll ease the pain."

"Aw, thanks..." Estelle said, and Lily nodded uneasily, clearly worried about the state Estelle was in. She noticed her agent's stress and tried to reassure her. "I'll be ready for the show when the time comes."

"How long did the doctor say it would take to heal?"

"Lil, I'll be alright. I just don't think I should be going out for any castings in the meantime."

"Oh, really? You think?"

Estelle nodded solemnly. "You can't tell Bianchi about this."

"What if you aren't healed in time? They'll need to find a replacement."

"Lily, I promise you. I'll be ready for it. I can't let someone else take my spot. Tell me you've never been in this situation before, where you've worked so hard for a spot in a major show..." Lily took in Estelle's plea, considering the request. Estelle added, "Please..."

Lily gave in. "I'm canceling every other Go-See I was planning on sending you out for. I'll check back with you in a week. If it's better, I won't mention it. Is that reasonable?" Estelle nodded thankfully. "No social media postings about this. Seriously."

"I know, of course."

Lily was quiet for a moment, watching Estelle. "You on your period? You're..." She motioned a finger around her face that said, *you're breaking out...*

Estelle sighed, letting her head fall back against the couch in frustration. "No, I think—I think I've just been really stressed lately..."

Lily nodded knowingly, understanding the situation Estelle was in, as a former model herself. She'd been trying so hard, working her ass off to get one step ahead, but was constantly met with another obstacle.

Lily became an agent for young models because she had been through it all, and felt like she could guide them with her knowledge and advice. She knew the industry from both ends now, and it was clear to her that Estelle was having a rough time of it. Yet, she kept pushing, determined to reach her goals. It was a great thing—a fantastic trait to have in the business. She just hoped that Estelle wouldn't end up burning herself out before any of it came into fruition.

***

Estelle bathed in Epsom salt while sifting through the magazines Lily had brought her. On the cover of Elle was Sofie in all her glory. Estelle flipped through her spread, reading only a few of the comments but mostly focusing on the photos of Sofie.

"Cunt," she said, her voice full of bitterness. She tossed the magazine to the side and picked up the next one.

Her face was the picture of depression: a mixture of anger, disappointment, and sadness. However, despite her despondence, she was still determined to be the best. Nothing would stop her.

Later in bed, she had her foot propped up and her laptop on her stomach as she scanned the homepage of Models.com. It was a website showing various ranking lists of models based on their successes, who was trending, who the top earners were, who was considered an industry icon, and so on. Sofie Tsai was the Model of the Year last year, at the age of seventeen. This year, she was currently in third place.

Estelle closed her eyes, willing her emotions away. She processed the information and let it fuel the fire that burned within her, urging her forward in her ambitions and career.

The next day she limped about her kitchen in a blue silk kimono, then leaned against the counter as she boiled an entire carton of eggs on the stove. She watched the bubbles rise and pop, zoning in on the clear pot with drooped, puffy eyes. She was utterly fatigued and her body felt weak. Her collar bones and rib cage across her chest were more pronounced than ever before.

The timer dinged, shocking Estelle out of her daze. She lifted the lid of the pot and spooned out each hard-boiled egg, one by one. Her feeble hand jittered as she spooned the last egg, and it rolled off the spoon, falling to the floor with a crack.

"Shit..." she breathed out with a sigh.

Once she had all the eggs peeled and prepped, she dished them into her Tupperware boxes labeled with every day of the week. Each contained one hard-boiled egg, one clementine orange, 12 baby carrots, and a tablespoon of peanut butter. The total caloric count for the week would be 1,255, or roughly 1,400 if all her black coffees were included.

She took the box labeled 'Monday' and headed to her couch, getting comfortable with her right foot resting on a pillow. Lifting her daily egg to her mouth, her eyes closed as she bit down and savored the flavor of the simple hard-boiled egg. It was a small pleasure to anyone else, but to her, it was the only indulgence she could have at that moment. Completely exhausted, she began to doze off, mid-chew.

When the sound of knocking on her door rang through the apartment, she jolted awake. Quickly lifting herself, she stood up and walked to the door. Before opening, she called out, "Who is it?"

"Hey, Estelle. It's Frankie D."

Frowning in confusion, she slowly opened the door to reveal Frankie D. himself standing in the doorway with a bouquet of cherry blossoms.

"Hey, sorry—did I wake you?"

"No, no. What are you doing here?"

"I was hoping to talk to you about something. Mind if I come in? Oh, these are for you."

She looked down at the flowers, still confused, but accepted them anyway.

"Oh, thank you..."

Opening the door wider, she stepped aside to let him in. Within a few minutes, they were seated next to each other on the couch, full wine glasses in hand and the cherry blossoms in a glass vase on the coffee table.

Frankie D. took a sip of the red wine, nodding with a tight smile. "Mmm... This is good. Where'd you buy this?"

Estelle's brows furrowed as she thought, *It's actually the shittiest wine you can buy... What's he playing at?*

"Good? You drink Johnnie Walker Blue. That's a two-buck Chuck from Trader Joe's. I steal it from my parents when I visit. I'm only 20."

He shrugged as if it made no difference to him, looking into his glass before taking another sip. "Well, it's good."

After an awkward silence, Estelle asked, "You wanted to talk to me about something?"

"Yeah... I don't know if you've heard, but I got brought on to shoot the next issue of Vogue."

She raised her eyebrows. "Congratulations..."

"I've shot a bunch of them before. It's just another gig."

"Well, you sound very excited."

He smirked. "If I remember correctly, you said your dream was to be on the cover of Vogue, wasn't it?" She nodded slowly, quietly fearing what might come next. "It's up to Anna who gets to be on the cover. But for this particular spread, we have multiple girls we're featuring. And I might just have one open slot if I find the right girl." Her heart stopped for a moment, skipping a beat. She stared, waiting for him to continue, to get to the punchline, to threaten her. But he just shrugged casually. "I might. It depends..."

Dreading his next words, Estelle asked carefully, "... On what?"

"On you."

Her shoulders dropped, and she looked at him incredulously. "Jesus Christ... You're asking me to blow you again?"

His smile was smug. "No, this is for Vogue. Bigger jobs tend to have bigger paychecks if you know what I mean. So, that's not gonna be enough." He slid closer to her on the couch, his thigh touching hers. She started to tremble. "I'm offering you this job. It's up to you whether or not you wanna take it. Who knows? You could actually end up on the cover if Anna likes you enough."

Estelle stared at her hands, wondering if her dream of being on the cover of Vogue was worth this much. *Who am I kidding? I've been dreaming of it since I was a child.* Eventually, she nodded—giving Frankie D. the green light.

He grinned sinisterly. "Just to be absolutely clear, you're saying 'yes' to this job offer..."

She nodded again, feeling completely ashamed of herself. He moved towards her, she let him pull her face to his, and he started kissing her lips. After a few moments of hesitation, she gave in, kissing him back.

Slowly he moved over her, pushing her down against the couch as he spread her kimono open to reveal her milky skin. His hands traveled over her waist, exploring her body and running up to her chest. The next thing she felt was his tongue slipping into her mouth, deepening the kiss.

Suddenly, his eyes jolted open and stared widely ahead. The veins in his neck and forehead swelled, looking as if they were about to burst. His voice careened out of his throat as he screamed loudly.

Estelle had the tip of his tongue between her teeth, biting down angrily. She snapped down harder, violently yanking and twisting like a frenzied piranha until his tongue was ripped from between his lips.

Blood gushed from his mouth and splattered onto her face. She pushed his body off of her, letting him fall flat on the floor as he seized up, bleeding out and choking on his own blood. She stood and looked back at her couch; it was covered in blood.

Breathing heavily, she rushed into her bathroom. Her feet were swollen—not from any sprain, however, rather a fat kind of swollen. She had cankles. She looked down at the faucet and splashed water onto her face, rinsing the blood from her mouth, before washing the blood from her hands. Her fat hands… *Wait, why are my hands fat?*

She looked up into the mirror. Staring back at her was a blood-drenched, triple-chinned, saggy-skinned, 300lbs version of herself. Her mouth dropped open in a desperate, blood-curdling scream.

Estelle's puffy, bloodshot eyes shot open as she jolted awake on the couch, screaming. Baby carrots from her Monday Tupperware spilled everywhere, onto the couch and onto the floor. Taking a few deep breaths, she calmed herself down.

It was only a nightmare… She closed her eyes, letting her heart rate simmer down as relief spread through her tense body.

***

Early in the morning, Estelle dragged herself out of bed. Leaning in towards the bathroom mirror, she poked a finger at her hollow cheeks and puffy eye bags. Turning to the side, she ran a hand down her ribcage, feeling each bone individually with an appreciative gaze as she looked herself over in the mirror.

She then applied her makeup, making sure to cover any remaining zits and dark eye bags thoroughly. She contoured her cheeks, adding color and character back to her face. Smiling faintly at herself, she continued on to her measuring.

She weighed 105.5 lbs. Closing her eyes, she nodded thankfully. *Another 2.5 lbs lost.* Her tape measurements were 31.5-21.5-31.5—an inch and a half lost all around. She shook her head. *I'm so close… Just not there yet.*

Wearing oversized sweatpants and a sweatshirt big enough to hide in, she walked steadily into the kitchen. Lily had promised to visit, and Estelle didn't want her to be even more concerned about her health. She was proud of the progress she'd made, losing inches, but she knew that her visible bones combined with her injuries and tired eyes made for a worrying sight. She needed to lose more if she was going to reach her goals, so she couldn't have Lily seeing her fragility and telling her she was going too far.

Her ankle wasn't fully healed but she was able to shuffle around her apartment, leaning on the furniture so she didn't put too much pressure on the sprain. She poured herself black coffee and reached into the fridge, taking her last Tupperware out, labeled 'Sunday.'

She headed to her couch and plopped down, lifting her feet into the footbath she'd prepared beforehand with Epsom salt in the water. There she relaxed and began to eat her daily meal. When Lily's knock on the door came, Estelle was expecting it.

"Hey, Lil. It's open!"

Lily entered and closed the door behind her. "Hey, how are you feeling?" Estelle saw that she was holding a bag of mini Reese's peanut butter cups.

"Ahhh, you're killing me. I don't wanna gain inches before the show!"

Lily chuckled and sat down next to her, waving the bag in the air. "Your favorite. You'll go crazy if you completely deprive yourself of everything. And about the show... How's your ankle? Your skin's looking better."

"Yeah, they've both gotten way better." Estelle lifted her foot up. The swelling was less significant and the color was almost back to normal. Her blisters had mostly healed.

Despite the improvements, Lily looked at her foot with doubt. "It's... better. Have you been able to put weight on that foot?"

"I haven't tried yet. I've just been letting it heal."

She nodded but pressed her lips together. "Hmmm, how can we be sure you'll be able to walk during the show?"

"'Cause I will be," Estelle said frankly, shrugging her shoulders and wishing Lily would just have some faith.

"Stelle, I can't go to Bianchi with, 'she'll be fine 'cause she says so.'"

"Do you wanna see me try to walk?"

"No, don't get up. Stelle, you have to understand that this is Bianchi's show, and he needs models who are gonna be at their best." Estelle pulled a slow breath in, trying not to feel let down, but was still disappointed that Lily couldn't trust that she'd be ready on time. Lily gently rubbed her thigh, "I'll see what they say and let you know as soon as I do. Okay?" She opened the bag of Reese's and tossed one to Estelle. "Here, have one. You'll feel better." Estelle was hesitant, but Lily unwrapped one and bit into it, talking again with a hand in front of her mouth to hide her peanut butter covered teeth. "You're not gonna gain inches from one. Trust me. You'll be fine."

Estelle slowly opened the wrapper and took a bite, savoring the flavor for as long as she could...

Because it was a short-lived pleasure. As soon as Lily left, Estelle made her way to the bathroom and shoved two fingers down her throat, puking it all up. Quickly re-measuring herself, she sighed a breath of relief. *Phew... No gains.*

***

The following morning, Estelle awoke and checked her phone. She had a list of Instagram notifications, but before checking anything else she tapped on the new email from Lily.

> *...he agreed to have an alternate on standby. If you can walk during rehearsals you're still in the lineup.*

She let out a relieved sigh. As long as her foot was metaphorically still in the door, she could prove herself.

Once up and about, she wrapped her ankle tightly in medical bandage, before easing her feet into her heels. Very, very slowly, she started to practice her walk again, being careful not to twist her ankle at all. Her face showed nothing but concentration while she did pass after pass, ten times over.

When a small stab of pain had her wincing, she sat down on the couch and removed her heels—replacing them with her running shoes. After a careful walk over to the gym, she worked on an elliptical machine. She managed fine at first but soon enough, fatigue crept in, faster than usual. She had to slow down and stop at only 3.3 miles, which was really more than enough because as soon as she stepped off the machine, her head began to spin. She leaned against the machine, catching her breath, and ended her workout with a slow walk off towards the locker rooms.

A woman who'd passed by Estelle on the machine had noticed her slow movements and ashen white face. When she entered the sauna not too long after, she almost gasped with fright when she came upon an exhausted, malnourished Estelle lying across the bench, looking like a starving victim of the Khmer Rouge. The woman averted her eyes and sat down. There wasn't much she could say to a stranger who was choosing to live this way.

Estelle's eyes were closed, and she tried to breathe steadily but the steam in the room became too much. With a spinning head and narrowing vision, Estelle stood up slowly and made her way to the showers.

Back at home, Estelle had recuperated somewhat and sat on her bed with a Korean sheet mask on her face when she received a forwarded email from Lily. It was the call sheet for the Bianchi show. After looking it over she quickly responded to Lily, confirming that she'd received it.

She then opened her Instagram and scrolled down through the hundreds of new likes and 104 new followers. Her total followers now sat at 21.1K. She smiled, encouraged by the support her fans showed, and with her sheet mask still on, quickly lifted her phone to film a short selfie video. With a cute smile, she stuck her tongue out ever so slightly between her lips, pulled a peace sign with her fingers, and then chose a pretty filter before posting it to her Instagram Story.

Chapter 9:

Alessandro Bianchi F/W

2021 Runway Show… and

Coffee

On the morning of the Alessandro Bianchi runway show, Estelle could hardly open her eyes. She didn't wake up on the first ring of her phone alarm, but rather floated into consciousness with a sharp sense of something important happening that day.

She dismissed the wailing alarm, then flopped onto her back again. Her eyes felt scratchy and dry, and her lips were chapped. Her energy levels were so low, she could have sworn they delved into the negatives. However, when her brain started functioning again, she remembered that she had to get to Vanderbilt Hall for Bianchi's show.

The stress of it pushed her out of bed and she stood in front of her bathroom mirror, assessing herself. Fortunately, her acne had cleared up and smoothed out. However, she looked skeletal. Her face was bony. Her torso was bony. Her butt was bony. She was altogether fuckin' bony. But Estelle only saw improvement.

She weighed herself—104 lbs. She measured herself—31-21-31. She gave herself a weak smile. *I've done it.*

Her ankle felt fine, and the swelling was barely visible anymore, but she wrapped it up tightly in medical bandage nonetheless. As she pulled her rain boots on, her phone vibrated next to her—Lily was FaceTiming her. She accepted the call hastily.

"Hey, I'm just about to head out."

Lily nodded appreciatively and delved into the information she'd just received from Bianchi's assistant. "So, the alternate's gonna be standing by during rehearsals. If Bianchi doesn't think you can walk, Chen Bingbing is gonna take your place. She's a hot new face from Shanghai and only 14."

Estelle stopped what she was doing, momentarily taken aback. "Bingbing? Her name is Bingbing? You serious? He has a 14-year-old named Bingbing who's trying to replace me? Bingbing probably doesn't even speak English, does Bingbing?"

Lily was quiet for a moment, hearing the utter bitterness in Estelle's voice. "Does that matter to you?"

"No—yeah... Did it have to be another Asian? Why couldn't they get a Russian girl or something?" Estelle sighed dramatically, but Lily was in no mood to indulge her.

"Just wow them during rehearsals. Get going. It's at noon. *Do not be late!*" She emphasized the last sentence, widening her eyes towards the camera lens.

"I'm on my way now. Thanks, bye!" Estelle waved quickly and put the phone down.

Under her umbrella, with her tote over her shoulder, Estelle paced down the street in jeans, an overcoat, and her bright yellow rain boots. It was a miserable day in terms of the weather and it didn't help her situation in the least.

On top of the crowds of umbrellas and honking traffic, she ran into a red light at *every single* intersection she came across. Every single motherfucking one. It heightened her anxieties bit by painful bit. At one of the red light stops, she checked the time. It was 10:37 a.m. *Fuck this.*

In her hurried state, she decided to cross the road—but as soon as she took a step down from the curb, a massive Big Bus Company tour bus came whooshing past and almost ran her over. She screamed and jumped back onto the curb, while herself and everyone around her was splashed with a giant wave of murky sidewalk rainwater.

Soaking wet, she eventually made her way down into the subway, where she rushed to the gates, zipped her Metrocard through the machine, and swiftly slammed into the unmoving barrier.

"What the fuck?"

She had insufficient funds on her card. With a growl of frustration, she turned and headed for the ticket machines, where she could recharge her card. Naturally, there were only two working machines and both had long lines. As she waited, tapping her foot, she impatiently checked the time again: 10:50 a.m. In front of her stood two Japanese tourists, probably in their forties. It was a man and a woman, and neither could figure out how to work the machine. Estelle leaned forward and caught their attention.

"Excuse me. Do you need help?"

The man replied to her in Japanese. "*I don't understand this thing.*"

Estelle lost her patience. "Motherfuck! Do you speak English? How much do you want to put onto your card? Where do you need to go?"

He looked around desperately, not knowing how to converse with her. "*Do you speak Nihon?*"

"What? I don't understand you. Does anyone know what language they're speaking? They need help. And I needa be on the train like yesterday."

A guy behind her in the line chimed in. "Just wait your turn, lady. Calm down."

She turned to him, fury in her eyes. "The line isn't gonna fuckin' move if they don't know what they're doing, asshole."

He challenged her with a raised eyebrow. "You're not related?"

"Oh, fuck you!"

A metro security guard approached them. "Everything okay over here?"

She gestured towards the tourists. "They don't know how to work the machine. No one here speaks their language, so we can't help them. And that dickwad over there is being a twat."

"Yeah, well you look like a bulimic coke head," the guy behind her added, as if he had a death wish that day.

"Fuck you!" Estelle shouted, and the guard held his hands out between them to settle the situation.

"Hey, hey, hey... You needa reload your card? Do it. I'll take them to a booth, and we'll get them taken care of."

Estelle glared at the guy hatefully before rushing to load her card. The time on the ticket machine read 11:01 a.m.

With a newly loaded card, Estelle rushed down the stairs, limping slightly now, just to see a glimpse of her train already picking up speed, heading off without her.

"Fuckin' shit…" she muttered, and tried to calm herself with the time she had. Only, with each second ticking by, her nerves tightened. She looked up towards the sign that read, "To Grand Central Terminal—Delay. ETA 11:46 a.m." The clock on the sign read 11:05 a.m. "You're kidding…" she groaned.

Still soaked with dirty rainwater, she began to sweat as she waited. At 11:10 a.m. her train finally arrived, and she pushed her way in, scrunched up between other passengers like sardines in a can. It felt to Estelle as if the train had never been slower. The doors took ages to close, the speed just wasn't fast enough, and the wait at each station felt like an hour.

Eventually, she jumped off the train cart at Grand Central. The clock read 11:54 a.m. Frantically she pulled out her phone and opened the call sheet sent to her via email—there were specific directions to the production office located at Vanderbilt Hall.

She looked up and saw a sign for Vanderbilt Hall—all the way on the other side of the station. She sprinted, grimacing from small stabs of pain with each pound of her foot. Sweat beads formed on her forehead, but, at 12:03 p.m., she found herself panting for air in front of the production office, which was under a pop-up tent outside of the hall.

She spotted the Production Coordinator, who without pause asked her, "What's your name?"

"Estelle Li."

She ran a finger down the list. "... Uhhh, oh, gotcha. Great. You're all set. Here's a badge that'll get you backstage access and anywhere we're set up."

"Okay?" Estelle said in a questioning tone, not sure in which direction she should be going.

"Head down the hall. You'll see the runway where all the other models should be right now for rehearsals. Just go. Hurry..."

"Okay, thank you..."

As she rushed into the venue, her eyes darted around. The entire room looked like George Tooker's *Bathers* trapped in an M.C. Escher-designed set. The runway was shaped like a long bathtub.

There were 50 models—all female. They stood in a line waiting for their instructions for the upcoming show. Estelle made her way to Bianchi's assistant who was holding a clipboard and wearing a headset.

"Hi, I'm so sorry I'm late..."

The assistant released a breath of relief. "Let's just get you into position. Quickly..."

Estelle was steered into the middle of the line, where she took a moment to look around her—she was the only model who was soaking wet and looked like shit. *Great.*

Bianchi's assistant held the button on the headset and spoke into it. "Estelle just flew in. I have her in her spot in the lineup." She then spoke to Estelle again. "I can take your things. We'll leave it on your makeup chair."

"Thank you."

As Estelle handed over her things, she caught a glimpse of Sofie, who stood at the front of the line talking to Bianchi himself. He glanced over, noticed Estelle, and quickly headed her way, while Sofie followed his gaze and saw her. Estelle glared at her, but Sofie turned away with a smirk on her face.

"You're late," Bianchi accused before he'd even reached her.

"I'm sorry. The train was—"

"You lost your spot to Bingbing."

"You can't be—are you serious? Over five minutes?" Her voice piqued with disbelief, but Bianchi shrugged.

"That's the reality of this business. There are consequences. You had your one chance. I didn't cut you when your agent told me you fucked up your ankle. I probably should have. But you can't even show up on time either. This is my show. I said you are out."

"But you haven't even started rehearsals yet. What's the big fuckin' deal?"

Models standing nearby were shocked at her tone, and they looked over with wide eyes. An equally shocked Bianchi was taken aback, before stepping towards her and speaking in a calm manner.

"The big fucking deal is you look like a fucking homeless person."

Estelle almost chuckled sarcastically, but managed to keep it in and spoke confidently. "Well, hey, you were the one who said heroin chic was back in Vogue, right?"

He was quiet for a moment, taking her words in and letting them linger in the air for a second. He then nodded and smirked. Her feistiness had brought him around.

"And what about your ankle? You think you can walk in my heels?"

"I know I can. Perfectly."

"Okay, we'll just see. If I notice even one tiny stumble during this rehearsal—even a little bit—you are out. I won't have anyone who isn't perfect ruining my show. Got it? Okay, good." He turned and shouted to his staff. "Get Estelle her heels!"

Estelle nodded confidently, ready for the challenge, while the assistant radioed the stylists for her heels.

Bianchi stepped onto the runway to address the room. "Everyone listen, listen. Now that everyone is here...

Just wanted to say we're going to have a great show. You are all amazing. I love you all. You're going to look fantastic, and we're going to celebrate afterward. Now... When you walk I want strong struts."

He demonstrated walking to the end of the runway. "When you get here, there are going to be all the photographers taking pictures and going crazy. Once you get here, I want you to stop, pose look right, pose look left, and continue turning and back down the runway. When you get to backstage you exit stage right. Okay? Everybody got it? Good. Line up backstage in the same order."

Everyone made their way backstage, and crew members watched on monitors as Sofie was first to be sent out onto the runway, practicing her opening walk. To no one's surprise, she was absolutely incredible, looking like an angel but without Victoria's Secret wings.

Waiting her turn, Estelle stood in the heels Bianchi had assigned her—noticeably higher than the rest. Coming up next, she took a deep breath in and put on a brave face. *This is the moment of truth.*

She took the runway step by step, watched by every pair of eyes in the room. It felt as if the silence of expectant onlookers was charged with the questions on everyone's minds: *Will she re-sprain her ankle? Will she sprain her left ankle instead? Will her balance go out? Will she fall?*

But there were no signs of any of the above. Not even signs of pain on her face. She looked relaxed, composed, walking flawlessly in the ridiculously high heels, and made it to the end of the runway. She did her poses as instructed, turned, and headed back.

When she arrived backstage, her eyes immediately searched for Bianchi. Their eyes met when he turned around to look at her, and after an insufferably long and tense moment, he nodded. *You're in.*

Turning away, she secretly breathed a quick sigh of relief as she realized—*it's happening. I'm really going to be in the show!* Her eyes dropped to her slightly swollen ankle, and she grimaced from the pain she'd refused to show on the runway.

When she reached the makeup room, she was led to her chair by a production assistant, Devyn. She looked to be very close to Estelle's age, and tapped her seat as she said, "I left your things on your chair."

"Thanks... Oh, since we have some time before the show, is there a big bucket I can use to soak my feet in while I'm getting my makeup done?"

"You need to soak your feet?" Devyn asked, pausing with a serious face.

"I know it sounds weird, but—"

Devyn lifted her hands innocently. "Oh, I'm not judging, I—I'll look and ask around and get back to you. Can I get you anything else though?"

"A black coffee would be great."

"Got it. Copy that."

Estelle took a breath of relief as she sat down in her chair. She was in pain. As Devyn headed out of the room, Sofie walked in holding a cup of coffee, stirring in her creamer with a stick. She sat down in her chair and looked over at Estelle next to her.

"How's your ankle?"

"Fine. Why?"

Sofie looked back down at her coffee. "Nothing."

"I'm sure Bingbing isn't happy about that," Estelle said flatly, eyeing herself in the mirror, but Sofie's eyes shot back up to her.

"Oh, Bingbing's still in the show. What they were planning on doing was taking your outfit and fitting it on her, so Bingbing would've had two outfits today."

"*Two* outfits?"

"You thought this was a single outfit show? Well, I guess it is for you but not for some of us."

"You have a second outfit?"

"I'm opening *and* closing the show."

Estelle tried to mask her jealousy but failed. The way Sofie boasted, it was as if she was acting like a spoiled girl, flashing her new toys in front of the poor kids. Or at least, that was how it felt to Estelle.

"Oh, well. Congrats."

"Thanks."

Devyn returned with Estelle's coffee, and stopped next to her. "Hey, Estelle. Here you go. So, no luck on the bucket. I'm sorry."

"Bucket?" Sofie asked curiously.

Estelle quickly looked at her, "Nothing!" She turned to Devyn again. "Hmm... Okay, thanks for the coffee."

"Of course. You need anything else?"

"I'm okay. Thank you."

Sofie quickly caught Devyn's attention. "It was Devyn, right?"

"Yup. What's up?"

Estelle rolled her eyes. *She remembers a fuckin' PA's name but not mine... Bitch!*

"Where's the restroom?"

"I can take you if you wanna just follow me..." The rushed Devyn started walking before finishing her sentence, so Sofie quickly jumped up to follow her, setting her coffee down on the table. As she did, Estelle noticed a tattoo on her right wrist. It was a small Chinese character: 蔡.

Wait, I didn't know she had a tattoo. Ah, whatever... Estelle glared at Sofie as she left, then glanced over at her makeup station, spotting her coffee. She thought for a moment, before looking around her and noting that all the models in the room had their heads down and eyes glued to their phones. She grabbed her tote and pulled out her travel-sized Epsom salt bottle.

Casually setting her own cup down next to Sofie's, she quickly took Sofie's coffee. She emptied the Epsom salt into the cup and stirred it in vigorously. Swiftly switching cups again, she made it just in time before the makeup artists filed into the room.

Lindsay was once again assigned to Estelle and Byrdie to Sofie. Lindsay gave Estelle a friendly smile. "Estelle... It's good seeing you again. How are you?"

"Hey... Couldn't be better." Estelle smiled, feeling nervous but slightly excited about the trick she'd just pulled. She felt a step ahead already.

"Lovely. Remind me, you're not allergic to anything, right?"

"Not that I know of."

Sofie re-entered the room and sat in her chair after hugging Byrdie hello. The pair started chatting about a bunch of nothing, while Estelle eagerly kept an eye on her coffee cup. Sofie picked it up… about to take a sip… when Byrdie distracted her.

"Look up here for a second..."

Sofie lowered her cup again as Byrdie applied something around her eyes, then reached back into her kit for something else. Given a moment between makeup applications, Sofie had time to take a sip of her coffee... then another sip... and... she was none the wiser. A devious smirk formed on Estelle's cheeks as she raised up her phone. *Selfie break!*

"Hey, everyone. Look over here!"

Sofie subtly rolled her eyes before switching to model mode, giving a wide range of poses from cute to sexy, but always looking effortless while doing so as Estelle snapped off about 20 snapshots.

Estelle grinned in excitement, "Amazing."

She then opened her Instagram, picked a photo, and did a quick edit before posting it with the caption:

> *Backstage at the Alessandro Bianchi runway show with the gorgeous @sofietsai and glam squad @byrdiemua @saylindsaymua.*

Immediately, there were a hundred likes and comments, with Estelle gaining 25 new followers within seconds.

Having tagged Sofie—an Instagram verified model—in her post, Estelle's following was boosted and every second she had the app open, she gained more followers. Her total count had reached 21.2K.

As Estelle was fitted into her outfit, she glanced across the room and saw Sofie being squeezed into a tiny waisted dress by two stylist assistants. Her face grew pale over a matter of minutes, and eventually, she looked almost green. The assistants began to notice her discomfort, and frowned in confusion.

She finally shook her head, with a look that said, *I'm gonna be sick…*

One of the assistants asked, "Are you okay?"

She answered frantically. "Get this off. Please, get this off…"

"What?"

"Please just get this off!"

Sofie covered her mouth and hunched over to retch. The stylists managed to get her out of the dress just in time, and in nothing but her undies, Sofie dashed out of the room, passing a smug-looking Estelle. Everyone in the room could hear Sofie puke before she made it to the restroom and looked around with wide eyes and confused faces, asking, "What's going on?"

"Is she okay?"

"What happened?"

Bianchi was freaking the fuck out. The assistant came out of the restroom and filled him in, while Estelle stood by within earshot.

"...Something is really wrong with her. She can't stop vomiting and..." She leaned in to whisper, "Runny diarrhea."

Bianchi pulled away with a disgusted face. "Are you fucking kidding me? Fine, we need to move on... Who only has one outfit?"

Both stylist assistants answered him, one with, "Bingbing." And the other with, "Estelle."

"Okay, get them fitted in Sofie's outfits now. *Now*, goddamn it!"

The assistants and other members of his stylist team immediately rushed to work. As Estelle was being fitted, she watched the young Bingbing during her fitting. She was tall, young, paper-thin, and clearly nervous. She was 14 but looked 25 with her makeup on. Breathing deeply, she was trying to calm herself down when Bianchi walked up and looked at both of them closely.

He pointed at Bingbing first. "You're going to open the show..."

Estelle went slack jawed. *What the fuck?* But then Bianchi pointed at her and said, "You're closing it."

Holy shit. Suddenly, Estelle was equally excited as she was nervous. The pressure was on, and the music started up as spectators began settling into their seats.

Chapter 10:

Madness and Disaster

Stage lights dimmed. The audience grew quiet. Camera, lighting, and sound crew members all focused their attention on the huge bathtub-shaped runway, while backstage Bianchi stood with the stage director with one eye on the monitor showing the runway, and the other on the models waiting to walk. When the time was right, the stage director signaled to Bingbing.

"Okay, ready, and… Bingbing, go, go, go!"

She stepped onto the runway, officially opening the show. If she was nervous, she certainly didn't show it. She was calm and collected as she strode like a seasoned vet. Audience members watched her carefully, assessing her outfit, appreciating her confidence.

Meanwhile, backstage was chaotic. People frantically ran around, yelling requests at one another over the loud, thumping music as they tried to keep the show running smoothly. Estelle stood in line, managing to be in her own head and trying to calm her nerves through light meditative calming breaths while an assistant tweaked small details on her outfit.

"Estelle!"

She heard Bianchi's voice and snapped back to reality. She stepped up to him at the entry to the runway and he looked her over one last time, then nodded to the stage director, confirming that she was ready to go. She closed her eyes, taking one last breath…

"Estelle, go!"

She was sent onto the runway, and her crazily high, high heels made their first few steps down the catwalk. Her face was blank, stoic, as she strutted fiercely down the catwalk. She tried to keep her gaze ahead of her, but when the iconic bob hairstyle and sunglasses of Anna Wintour materialized in her peripheral vision, she couldn't help but sneak a casual sideways peak.

Oh my God. Anna Wintour's here. Is she watching me? She's watching me…

Next to her sat Frankie D. His gaze was locked solely onto Estelle, even as she crossed paths with the model ahead of her, and made her way to the end of the runway.

When she stopped to pose left, her eyes swayed back to Anna, and she was surprised with the faces of Blackpink sitting alongside her.

Holy shit… That's Jisoo! And Jennie… Lisa… and Rosé!

She kept her cool but was freaking out on the inside. When she posed right, her eyes landed on a few more famous faces. *That's A$AP Rocky. And is that… a Kardashian? What did she do to her face? Nevermind. Who* *cares. Focus. Focus. Focus.* Feeling the weight of the moment, Estelle walked back with heightened anxiety.

When she made it backstage she closed her eyes for a brief moment as adrenaline rushed through her veins. The assistant appeared at her side asking, "Are you okay?" Estelle opened her eyes and nodded uneasily. "Alright, hurry. Let's get you changed."

She was rushed off to the changing room and hastily shoved into her closing outfit. The adrenaline from a moment ago had worn off, and she felt a whack of fatigue hit her. They carefully slipped the delicate cherry blossom swim cap over her head while she swayed back and forth like a giant, inflatable tube man, standing in the middle of a seven-person whirlwind around her, zipping, pulling, sewing. She began to feel her sight tunnel-visioning.

The room spun around her as the extremely tight outfit was being finalized while on her body. It might as well have been a corset, it was so tight. She struggled to breathe.

"Where is Estelle? We're near the end! I need her back here *now*!"

Bianchi shouted and the style crew looked nervously in his direction as they worked faster, before rushing her over to him. Her cue was only seconds away while they were still sewing the outfit onto her body—it was madness.

Bianchi fidgeted with her waistline, talking to the seamstress. "This needs to be tighter. Hurry up."

Estelle pulled a deep breath in… Well, as much as she could with the dress squeezing the life out of her. It didn't help. The dress was too tight.

"Okay good," Bianchi stepped back. "Beautiful."

"And… *Go!*" The stage director signaled with his hand then pushed her out onto the runway.

Strutting straight ahead, she began to feel overwhelmed. The constant flashes of the photographers blinded her, and she struggled to see as her vision tunneled again. Luckily, she managed to make it to the end of the runway. She posed, swaying slightly, then turned to head back.

She was almost there, almost done, so close to the finish line, when she stopped in the middle of the runway. Something was wrong. The audience started mumbling, *What's she doing…*

She couldn't see. She was lightheaded, her consciousness fading away. Her knees began to shake, her ankles followed suit, and next, the insanely high, high heels wobbled as her eyes rolled to the back of her head. Her body gave out and hit the runway along with a wave of shocked cries and gasps from the audience. Meanwhile, photographers and social media influencers in the crowd snapped pictures of her, recording her collapse like a pack of ruthless parasitic leeches.

***

Bianchi rushed down the runway to her side, checking if she was okay before shouting out for someone to call emergency medical assistance. He lifted her head and started fanning her face. He'd seen models faint before, but not like this. This was something else. She was pale, she almost looked dead. He suddenly thought back to his comment about her looking like a fucking homeless person, and felt like perhaps that was a red flag he should have addressed.

Later, he stood backstage with his team. Everyone was wondering and asking each other, "How did this happen?"

He was too frustrated to respond. All he could do was think back… *The original plan was for Sofie to close my show. Sofie would not have collapsed. Sofie looked great during rehearsals. Sofie was ready. But then… Sofie has to go off and fucking disappear into the fucking restroom only minutes before my fucking show was supposed to fucking open…* "Fuck!"

***

Estelle's eyes slowly blinked open and adjusted to the bright lights. She was lying in a hospital bed, with her mother and sister at her side. Her father was pacing the room with crossed arms. He stopped and looked up when a doctor entered the room.

"Ms. Li… I'm Dr. Park. Do you know where you are right now?"

137

Estelle mumbled, "Why—why am I—what's going on?"

Her sister put a comforting hand on hers. "You collapsed on the runway."

In sheer confusion, Estelle frowned. "What?"

"Ms. Li, you can't continue doing what you're doing. You're completely underweight and malnourished. The tests we ran show that your body's deficient and lacking every possible vitamin and nutrient that we know of."

"I didn't finish the show?" Estelle asked, still disorientated.

The doctor shook his head. "You're lucky you didn't die. I'm going to have a nutritionist talk to you about a new diet plan I want you to get on. You need to take it easy. Rest. Eat. It's that simple. Got it?" He turned to her family. "She'll be okay. We do need to keep her here for at least a few days in order to monitor her."

"A few days?" Christian asked. "Is that really necessary?"

"Another model—14-year-old girl from Russia—also collapsed on a runway three months ago. She went into a coma and died two days later. Better safe than sorry." He shrugged and left the room as a nurse entered.

"Hi, sorry... So, visiting hours are now over. You can come back and see her again tomorrow morning. Earliest at 8 a.m."

Estelle was still processing what happened, when her mom leaned down and spoke to her with desperation.

"When I was in the labor camps in Cambodia, we worked all day in the fields while the Khmer Rouge were starving us to death... You're here in America with all the food options in the world to choose from, and you've been choosing to starve? I just don't understand..." May kissed Estelle on the forehead and she dropped her head back, staring off blankly.

As her family was being led out by the nurse, Richard stopped at the door and took one last look at Estelle. He was heartbroken but suppressed his emotions with a sad shake of his head. When she was alone, Estelle's eyes welled up with tears. She broke down crying, feeling the complete and utter disappointment of her failure crash down onto her.

***

After being released from the hospital a few days later, Estelle was helped back to her apartment by her family. Christian held her arm as she lowered herself on the couch.

"Me and muh-mii are gonna go to the store and pick up what's on this list for you. Call us if you need anything."

Estelle nodded, and Christian and May left. She was now alone with her father, who stood awkwardly before asking, "Do you want me to make some tea?"

She didn't answer, she didn't even hear him. Her mind was too busy swimming in emotions, in the tsunami of

events that had brought her to that point in her life—
malnourished and at the mercy of her family. After
pulling her gaze away from her wall of inspiration, she
swallowed deeply and looked up at her father. "What
do I have to do to make you proud of me?"

Richard was not expecting that. He sighed and took a
seat next to her on the couch. The words he spoke next
were in Mandarin—something he very rarely did with
Estelle.

*"Listen to me carefully. In Asian families, we don't always have
to say we're proud of our kids, even if we are. Just like we don't
have to keep saying, 'I love you,' all the time. We already know
it."*

Richard let it linger, before continuing.

*"I know you think I just want you to go back to school... Of
course, I'd prefer that... But do you think I don't notice how
passionate you are or how hard you work at your modeling? Of
course, I'm proud of that. Of course, I'm proud of you."*

Estelle's lips began to quiver with raw emotion. She
couldn't remember a time when her father had been
this open, this honest with her.

*"It's just that, where I come from, a passion isn't a career, and I
don't like seeing my daughter struggling all the time for something
that's still just a passion right now. No father—Black, White,
Chinese, Mexican, old, or young—wants to see their kid working
as hard as you do and still struggling, hoping that one day they'll
turn this passion into a career. Am I right?"*

Tears built in Estelle's eyes.

"If you want to make it in the fashion industry you have to be tough, okay? Stop crying."

She immediately wiped her tears, while Richard walked over to his coat and pulled out the latest issue of the Chinese Newspaper, handing it to her.

"This might not mean anything to you, but a lot of Chinese people will see this. That's not nothing."

Estelle opened it up—on the front page was the most unflattering photo of her, sprawled out on the Bianchi runway floor. There were blurred people around her, some staring down at her motionless body, others running and calling out to each other.

The Chinese headline read, *"Chinese fashion model Estelle Li, 20, collapses during Alessandro Bianchi's runway show."*

Estelle glanced at Richard with a half-smile, nodding appreciatively. He gently patted her on the thigh, which was as much affection as anyone would ever get from an Asian parent. She understood his sentiment and was truly happy that he was being so understanding and supportive. However, as she looked back down at the newspaper, her true feelings shone in her eyes.

What a disaster… What a complete nightmare.

Chapter 11:

Verified ✔

A tired, red-eyed and disgruntled Sofie sat at the police station, giving her statement.

"Someone had to have done something—put something in my food."

"How?"

"I don't know... I didn't even eat anything." She shrugged, tears threatening to fall again.

She was still trying to figure out what had happened herself, so she didn't have much to tell the police. She recalled only having a banana in the morning before making her way to Vanderbilt Hall, and some quinoa for dinner the night before to avoid the potential of being bloated during the show itself. Neither of these could've affected her body like this.

She could only imagine that something had to have happened at the show, and that she had been way too busy getting ready that she didn't notice.

"If you didn't eat anything, how could someone have—"

"Because, Officer, one second I was fine, and the next I was throwing up. That doesn't make any sense." She ran a frustrated hand through her hair, sighing and looking around the room.

The policeman looked her over, not sure what he could even do about her claims. "Look, honey. I wanna believe you. But without any evidence to go on, there's nothing I can do."

Her shoulders drooped, and she nodded solemnly. She'd have to figure this one out by herself...

***

Dark roast coffee steamed as it was poured into two cups—one for Estelle and one for Lily. They were seated at Katie's Kafé, a hip brunch spot on a busy Manhattan street. Estelle had taken a few more days to recover, and was now feeling more energetic, but less like herself than ever.

"I actually turned off my Instagram notifications and haven't been online since it happened. I'm afraid of seeing how mean people can be. I've actually been thinking a lot about going back to school..."

Lily knew she'd been through a difficult time, but she needed Estelle to refocus and toughen up again if she was ever going to make it in the industry. "You know, every top model has fallen on the runway before. It's not the worst thing that can happen."

Estelle shook her head in disagreement. "Have you ever fallen during a major runway show?"

Lily sat back with a solemn face. "I have, actually. It was also during a haute couture show. The dress I was in was long and pencil-thin. My heels got caught in it... and I fell." She let that linger in the air, watching Estelle.

"I was just lucky I didn't have the internet back then where everybody in the world instantly knew about it. I'm the only agent at Ford who used to be a model. Believe me, I've been through it all. I've actually walked the walk... many times. And I don't even know how many times I've been told, 'You're too fat. You're not tall enough. Your face shape is weird.' Negative, negative, negative. That constant negativity broke me, and I don't want that to happen to you. I know it's difficult but try not to be discouraged by hardships and failure. Work even harder instead. If you need anything, I'm here. I wanna be a strong support system for my girls because I never had that when I was modeling."

Estelle was quiet for a moment, letting Lily's words simmer in her mind. "Do you regret it? Quitting..."

Lily glanced down, her eyes searching, reflecting. They were the eyes of a former dreamer. "Sometimes, but that doesn't mean you have to. You know, it's not every day I hear from a major couture designer that he thinks one of my girls could be the next Kate Moss... But are you asking me or are you really asking yourself that question?" Estelle pondered her question quietly. "Seems like you know the answer..."

Estelle sighed before nodding sadly. *I would regret it...*

"So, when's my next Go-See?"

Lily started off slowly. "You're not gonna like this, but after what happened to you, no designer or brand is willing to take the risk of hiring anyone your size again. At least not for a while. They don't want the backlash and negative press."

Estelle frowned. "Wait, for four years since I've been modeling, everyone in this business has pushed me to, 'lose inches, lose inches, lose inches...' You've even told me I needed to lose inches. Now you're saying no one's gonna hire me unless what? I *gain* inches?"

"Well, to be clear, those weren't my opinions about you. I was just telling you what clients are telling me about what they're looking for. Just like I'm telling you now how you would need to gain inches, otherwise, they won't even consider hiring you."

Estelle furrowed her brows. *What the fuck...*

"And listen, even though I'm your agent, I hope you know that I care more about you than I care about you being a model. The reason I want you to succeed is that I know how passionate you are. If success equals happiness for you, I'm happy for you. And if you decide to quit and go back to school, you'll be dead to me."

That lightened the mood, and Estelle laughed with Lily before sighing tiredly. "So, now I needa gain inches. Great..."

"Since the Bianchi show, every client I hear from is saying, 'We want girls with healthy-looking bodies now.'"

A server appeared next to them, dropping off a large plate of pancakes. Estelle looked down, almost unable to believe that she could suddenly indulge, and not feel guilty about it.

While replying to Lily's comment about what clients suddenly want, she slowly picked up her fork. "God, I hate when people say that. What does that even mean? How much do they want girls to weigh? What measurements do they want us to be?"

Lily thought for a moment, before telling Estelle calmly, "I'm sure that any inches you gain will be a good start." She slid the pancakes on the table over to her. "Yeah?"

Estelle stared at the pancakes for a few moments before cutting into them, reluctantly accepting her new task of gaining inches. It felt like going back to square one.

"Hey, I heard there's a new Japanese place in Lower Manhattan where they serve fluffy soufflé pancakes. You and Sam should check it out sometime."

Estelle paused suddenly, not meeting Lily's eyes but instead looking downward with a face of pure regret.

***

Later, Estelle sat on her balcony with a cigarette. She stared off into the distance, absentmindedly holding her glass of wine tightly. The smoke from the cigarette wafted upward, swirling around her head in the breeze. Her eyes glistened with tears, but a slight smile grew across her lips. She was trying so hard to hold herself together while pasting the smile on as a protective façade.

She ended up in the tub, soaking in Epsom salt again, except this time she had a giant bowl of Reese's peanut butter cups and a blender filled with green juice, packed with nutrition, on the floor next to her. She was eating the peanut butter cups to gain inches while the green juice was meant to counter the massive sugar intake. At least that was the idea in her head and her way of convincing herself that it was okay to be so unhealthily indulgent.

She reached down, grabbed a Reese's cup, and stuffed the entire thing into her mouth. As she chewed her eyes narrowed in thought, causing her to quickly reach for her phone. She typed her own name into the Google search bar.

A list of articles appeared, but she zeroed in on one, in particular, titled, *"A model's worst nightmare... #thinsperation gone too far..."*

It felt like a kick to the gut. She turned her head and glanced at herself in the mirror. Staring back at her was a young girl, filled with self-pity and hatred. She pulled her gaze away and took a deep breath in, bracing herself for what came next: internet trolls. She was going to check her Instagram account for the first time since her collapse.

She touched the Instagram app icon. It began to load... Suddenly her brows furrowed... *Wait? Am I seeing this correctly?*

She had a notification for 55K new followers, with hundreds of thousands of likes and comments. She sat up in the tub, scrolled through the comments, and to her surprise, found the majority to be positive.

Her followers and fans were being kind, encouraging, and supportive. She was suddenly at a loss for words, struggling to believe what she was seeing. Completely taken aback, she merely gaped at the growth of her following and the number of supportive people who only wanted her to be happy and healthy again.

***

It was early evening when Estelle was seated at a table that ran along the storefront of a popular pizza shop, with a view out onto the noisy street. She sprinkled parmesan cheese over a slice of cheesy pepperoni pizza, while the rest of the large pizza waited to the side.

A quiet, careful Sam sat next to her. She stuffed the slice into her mouth, taking a large bite and pulling the pizza away to break the string of cheese hanging from her lips. She looked over at Sam.

"You're not hungry?"

He shook his head. "I'm good."

That's unusual... "Well, feel free to have some if you want."

"Thanks."

"You're welcome." She smiled happily and casually shifted her body so that her knee touched his. He moved his knee away. Disconnecting from her physically, and clearly, psychologically. Her brow furrowed, but she tried to hide her confusion. She knew that she had some apologies to make. Sam cleared his throat and awkwardly spoke up.

"So, um, yeah... How've you been? I was really worried about you when I saw what happened."

"Oh, uh... Yeah, no. I'm fine. It really wasn't a big deal like people made it out to be... On a new diet plan now, which requires a lot more eating, obviously." She glanced at the pizza, hoping to entice him. "That's always fun, right? How about you?"

"Yeah, I've been pretty good. Got two different job interviews lined up. Guess I should thank you for that."

She swallowed her food. "I did that?"

"Well, what you said when you were—"

"Yeah, you didn't deserve to be treated that way. I feel so terrible about that..."

Sam read the look in her eyes and deciding it was indeed genuine, nodded with a tight smile. "No, but you were right though, and so, yeah. It is what it is now."

She pulled in a quiet breath, bracing herself for what she came here to ask. "So, are you... like, maybe interested in..." She subtly gestured between them, her finger finishing her sentence for her: *giving us another chance?*

Sam clenched his jaw, not looking very happy. "You said you had goals and ambitions and I was getting in the way of that." He looked out onto the street, thinking back. "It was always about you and your modeling..."

"I really wanna apologize for that."

Sam sighed, his face clearly saying: *I guess there's no easy way to say this.* "I've actually, kinda, been seeing someone. I'm meeting her for dinner after this."

Estelle was shocked silent for a moment, feeling hurt and disappointed. She hadn't expected him to have moved on so quickly. She plastered on a fake smile, wanting him to think she was fine with it, when in actuality she was freaking out on the inside.

"Oh, awesome—great, um... Where are you guys going? Yeah, you know, you're right. It's probably for the best. It wouldn't be fair to you anyway 'cause I'm still focusing really hard on my career, so... Yeah, I mean, now's the time." She rambled on, letting her words fill the space between them. "Especially because people are really starting to know who I am now. D'you know I've gained more followers in a week than I previously had in total on Instagram? Have you seen my profile lately? Lemme show you..."

She pulled her phone out and opened her Instagram, leaning over to show him. She wanted him to see that she was doing well, that she was thriving now. She had 112K followers and a blue verification checkmark.

"Look, I'm verified now. Supposedly, Instagram's the hardest social media platform to get verified on. So, yeah... Sorry, where were you guys having dinner again?"

She stopped herself by stuffing her face again. With her mouth still full, she began shaking Parmesan on top of her next slice.

Sam just looked at her, unsure how to respond.

Chapter 12:

Blacklisted

Estelle's goals were still the same—to become a top model. But everything felt different. Suddenly, she was indulging in food to gain inches, instead of losing them. She was resting her body, instead of working on it. She knew she was doing what she needed to, but it just felt wrong.

The sun had set on the horizon, and the nightlife was breaking free outside her windows. She could hear excited shouts and laughs of young people heading out to party, but walked over and closed her window. She was in her bathroom, once again checking her measurements. It wasn't like she needed to; it was more out of obsessive curiosity.

Her completely healed feet stepped onto the scale one by one. She weighed 108 lbs. She pulled off her sheer white kimono so she could measure her torso. She was now at 33-23-33. She gained four pounds, and two inches all around.

Reluctantly she lifted her gaze and stared at her naked body in the mirror, with pure self-hatred in her eyes. Turning to her side, she pushed her gut out.

"You look like a fucking disgusting, fat fucking fuck, but… They want you to gain inches now. You fuckin' need to gain inches now… Gain inches, gain inches, gain fuckin' inches!"

Estelle angrily grabbed a two-pack of Reese's she had lying on the counter and stuffed one right after the other into her mouth, barely even chewing as she watched her reflection gorge herself. It didn't feel real.

Pulling her kimono back on, she flopped onto her couch and took out her phone to check her Instagram comments. An hour had passed without her realizing when there was a knock on her door.

"Who is it?"

"Hey, it's Frankie D."

Estelle frowned. *Something feels like a déjà vu here…* "Uhhh, hang on a sec…"

She stood up, tied her kimono, and cracked open her door, peering outside. Frankie D. was truly standing there holding a bouquet of cherry blossoms and a bottle of wine.

"Hey…" She said uneasily.

"Hi." Frankie D. greeted curtly but gave her a quick smile.

"How do you know where I live?"

"I spoke to your agent—"

"You? You talked to Lily?"

"Well, Carson did... Is this a bad time?" He looked down at the flowers and wine. "Oh, these are for you, by the way."

She opened the door wider and let him in while he handed her the cherry blossoms. He held onto the wine.

"Thanks... You know I'm not legally allowed to drink, right?"

He looked around her place, his eyes touching every detail, and lingering on her wall of inspiration. "When has that ever stopped you?"

She shrugged. *Touché...* "You can... have a seat. What are you doing here?"

Estelle set the cherry blossoms on the coffee table and gestured for Frankie D. to take a seat on the couch, then quickly stepped into the kitchen and grabbed two wine glasses.

Frankie D. spoke while she was busy, raising his voice so she could hear from the kitchen. "I was at Alessandro's show—"

"I saw you," she said, walking back in and setting the wine glasses on the table. He popped the bottle open and started pouring.

"Well, I just wanted to come by and see how you were doing, how you were feeling... Cheers—" He raised the glass for a toast but slowly lowered it when she responded back with an icy tone in her voice.

"Really? Mister I-like-lipstick-stains," she glanced down. "... cares how I'm feeling? Why are you really here?" She eyed him with suspicion while refusing to clink glasses.

Obviously, she didn't trust the man. Yet... because of his stature, his connections—his power, she gave him the time of day. She slowly took a sip of wine, watching him carefully. He put his lips on the rim of the glass, but stopped and looked at her instead.

"You know, Alessandro blames Sofie for the failure of his show. Not you. If she hadn't been sick, she would've closed the show, and what happened to you would've never happened. He wants her blacklisted."

"Oh... What a shame. How is she?" Estelle pretended to care. Well, she definitely did, but in the opposite way than what she was portraying.

"You haven't heard? Word around town is she went to the police..."

She frowned, suddenly perking up. "Wait, really? Why?"

He casually leaned back against the couch and lifted one of his legs over the other. "She thinks somebody food poisoned her at the show or something crazy like that. But unless she has proof, the cops aren't actually going around investigating a food poisoning claim. She could've gotten sick from anything in the days leading up... Plus, girls shouldn't be eating before a runway show anyway, right?"

Relieved, Estelle took another sip of wine, while Frankie D. set his glass down. "Anyway... Anna and her team are starting to work on this year's September issue. They said she's looking for the next 'non-White It Girl' to be on the cover. Their words, not mine... And the entire issue's gonna be about diversity 'cause everyone's fuckin' obsessed with that and skin color and race and gender and all that other bullshit no one in the real world actually gives two shits about... But the plan is to do a spread with all the top models of every color and one of them is gonna be on the cover."

Estelle was quiet, but when Frankie D. didn't say anything else she asked, "Okay? So, why are you—"

"Your name came up."

Her eyes lit up. *Wait, what... Anna Wintour knows my name?* "It did?"

"But so did your size."

Of fucking course.

"I've already gained two inches on all my measurements, plus four pounds since the show."

"Well, that's good to know 'cause it just so happens that Anna brought me back on to shoot this very spread.

Plus, I have a stipulation in my contract that says I have a say in which girls are cast in this."

Estelle eyed him, processing his words. She immediately knew where he was going with this.

"So, tell me... Wasn't it your dream to be in Vogue?"

She stared at him with cold eyes, feeling like she was frozen in place. Out of fear? Or out of her own volition? Because she was the one who wanted what he was offering, she was the one not kicking him out right now.

"Since Sofie's now off everyone's list... I need a different Asian."

He watched her patiently, quietly. He'd made his offer, and the rest was up to her now. Estelle thought for what felt like a lifetime before she gulped down the rest of her wine, and set the glass down on the table. She sat back, then reluctantly turned her body to face him, and slowly untied her kimono.

Frankie D. smiled coolly before sliding in closer to her. He then pulled her face in for a kiss, reminding her of his stench. This wasn't the kind of stench caused by bad hygiene. This 'stench' was something only the girls he'd taken advantage of would be able to describe. Estelle was still rigid with tension but tried to relax her body as he pushed her downward, and spread open her kimono. With an appreciative look at her white body, he licked his lips and moved on top of her. As his face moved closer to hers, he stuck his tongue out towards her mouth.

She suddenly lifted her head and bit his tongue, ferociously clamping down onto it like a bear trap— *No... I shouldn't...* She pushed the imaginary scene out of her mind.

Her eyes shifted back and forth between his, considering her possible actions as he moved closer... and closer... She stared directly at his tongue. The closer it got, the larger it became... So close now, it almost touched her when she suddenly pulled away, pushing her hands up against his shoulders.

"No... No—stop. I—I can't..."

Frankie D. leaned back, annoyed. *What. The. Serious. Fuck...*

He sighed, throwing a hand into the air. "Guess you don't wanna be in Vogue that badly after all."

Estelle breathed hard as she considered his words... Suddenly, her head felt ten times lighter. She was hit with a strange wave of wooziness and blinked a few times, trying to remain conscious.

Frankie D.'s brows furrowed and he put a hand on her shoulder as he lowered her back down onto the couch. "Hey, what's wrong? Take it easy. Just lie back. You okay?"

She was not. She started dozing off as her eyes rolled back, and Frankie D. watched her with what seemed to be concern before his face relaxed. His eyes traveled down her exposed body. His tongue licked his lips again, and his head moved lower and lower... until his face disappeared into her crotch.

Unmoving on the couch pillow, her head tilted to the side and her eyes landed on the coffee table, on the bottle of wine, on her empty glass...

...and on Frankie D.'s full glass of wine, completely untouched.

***

A sharp ray of sun warmed Estelle's cheek. She groaned, putting her hand over her eyes to block out the bright light. *God, why is my head throbbing so hard...*

She braved the sun and fluttered her eyes open. She was in bed. *Was last night a dream? So strange...*

Suddenly, a wave of nausea hit her and she jolted out of bed, making it to the toilet bowl just in time to puke. Her stomach wrenched until she had nothing more to expel from her body. Completely weak, she rested her head against the toilet seat until she felt the strength to lift herself up.

Why do I feel so hungover?

She walked into her living room and looked around. No cherry blossoms, no wine bottle, and no wine glasses anywhere in sight. She frowned, rubbing her forehead to ease the throbbing headache. *What happened? Was I...*

With a growing sense of panic, she sat down on the couch and pulled her underwear down to inspect herself.

***

Later in the day, Estelle walked through the foyer of Ford Models, into the office, and was met with immediate applause from all the agents. Some came forward to hug her and shake her hand while she stood wide-eyed.

"What's going on?" She asked, and Lily appeared at her side, squeezing her shoulder.

"Vogue called this morning. They asked if you'd like to be featured as one of the main girls in the spread for the September issue. I said, 'yes.'"

Estelle couldn't believe what she was hearing. "Seriously?"

Lily handed her a bundle of flowers. Overwhelmed, she didn't notice they were the same cherry blossoms Frankie D. brought her the night before. Everyone hugged her, creating more of a distraction until Lily pulled her away and sat her down in the lounge area.

"Your dream. It's happening... Vogue said they heard you've gained inches."

Estelle nodded, wondering how they knew. "Two inches on all measurements plus four pounds."

"No kidding?" Lily smiled, looking happy for Estelle. "Well, we'll shoot a video of us taking your measurements later and send it to them. Just so they can know for sure you've gained... You see, hard work doesn't go unnoticed. I'm really proud of you."

Estelle chuckled, "It's weird. I still can't believe this. Thank you for believing in me."

"We thought you already knew. When his assistant called, I gave her your info because she said Frankie D. had good news he wanted to tell you himself in person."

"He did?" Estelle thought for a quiet moment, before mumbling to herself, "So, that wasn't a dream...?"

"What wasn't a dream?"

"Feels like déjà vu. I'm just thinking I could've sworn Frankie D. came over to my apartment last night with these exact same cherry blossoms and a bottle of wine, which I also could've sworn having a glass of. Weird thing is, I didn't see any flowers or wine bottle in the morning, so I just thought it was a bad dream... But I still don't get why I felt super hungover right when I woke up."

Lily looked unsure. "I don't know anything about that bottle of wine you're referring to, but his assistant dropped these flowers off this morning. And I think I'm still a little confused as to what you're getting at."

It started to dawn on Estelle, and she spoke carefully, trying to remember every detail. "I'm starting to think it wasn't a bad dream. I think something actually happened to me last night."

"What are you talking about?"

"I don't even wanna say... I think Frankie D. put something in the wine then did something to me after I must've passed out. He had to have cleaned up 'cause I looked around this morning and everything seemed in place. But you ever get that feeling when you just know something isn't right? Something just feels off?"

"Jesus Christ..." Lily looked around the room, before locking her serious gaze on Estelle again. "Are you sure about this? Have you told anyone else?"

"No, I thought it was a dream 'cause I've had really, really horrible dreams in the past, so—but now... I really don't think it was..."

Lily leaned forward, speaking in a low and serious tone. "Okay, I want you to listen to me. You needa go to the police to get a rape kit done. If he did what you think he did, you'll have proof. And if it turns out he really did this to you, there's a good chance he's probably done this to other girls too."

Estelle thought hard, then started to shake her head. "But if I do, I could lose the Vogue shoot..." Being in

Vogue was her ultimate dream. How could she throw it all away for something she wasn't even entirely sure had happened?

"This is bigger than just a Vogue shoot."

"Just a Vogue shoot? Being in Vogue and possibly on the cover has been what I've been working towards since I started modeling. I can't risk losing this job. Let's just forget I ever mentioned this. Okay?"

Lily watched her with her mouth slightly agape, trying to comprehend what Estelle was saying. *She's going to forget it happened? She won't even consider thinking more about it?* Lily's fears might have been materializing after all—Estelle was letting her modeling career take priority over her own well-being. Possibly the well-being of a few other models out there as well, and more importantly, models still to come if Estelle wasn't going to report him.

"Lil, you can't tell anyone I told you this. If he finds out, he'll blacklist me the way he and Bianchi just blacklisted Sofie. And now that she's out of the picture, this is my opportunity to be the top Asian fashion model in the world."

Lily quickly raised a hand, "Wait, what do you mean Sofie is being blacklisted? Who told you that?"

"Frankie D.… Last night. I think."

"Estelle... "

"Please, just—Lily, just forget I ever said anything, okay? Please..."

Lily was completely taken aback with no words to say. *I can't believe what I'm hearing...*

Chapter 13:

Gooey Peanut Butter Cups

Seated comfortably on her couch, Estelle felt excited as she searched previous Vogue spreads and covers on her laptop. She was doing her research, reminding herself what Vogue would want from a cover model when Lily's FaceTime call flashed in the corner of her laptop screen.

She answered and smiled. "Hey, Lily."

"Hey, so Frankie D. wants to do a pre-shoot at the studio tomorrow for a hair, makeup, and costumes test to make sure everything looks the way it should before the actual shoot."

"Okay."

"It's supposed to be minimal crew. Glam, his photo assistants, and some Vogue reps..."

"What about the other models?"

"You'll all have staggered call times, so they can shoot each of you out."

"Okay. Have they already sent out the call sheet?"

Estelle was in business mode, ready for it, but Lily was still not convinced that she was truly okay. She paused and pulled in a deep breath.

"Stelle, it's still not too late to go to the police."

Estelle sighed and shook her head, "Lil..."

"It's also not too late to get a rape kit done. If he's really a predator, drugging and raping girls, you can help put a stop to this. Think about how many lives he's probably destroyed and how many girls you might just save from him."

Estelle thought her words over. "You know what? That's on them. If girls are gonna let a single incident destroy the rest of their lives or allow a creep like Frankie D. to stop them from getting to the top... Well, then they just don't have what it takes to be a top model anyway."

Lily was quiet on her end... Once again at a loss for words.

***

Sitting in front of the mirror in the makeup room, Estelle was having her crazy-looking 'high-fashion' hair and makeup done. It was the day of the pre-shoot, and she felt like royalty already—amongst some of the best, top of the top models. And, not just the top models from America… but the top models from around the world too. Somehow that made her feel even more special and successful.

Frankie D. popped his head into the room, acting as if nothing ever happened between them. As if he didn't just Bill Cosby her ass the other night.

"Hey... How's it looking?"

"Great, like Puddin' Pops... Thanks again for having me on this. And for the flowers you sent to Ford."

Estelle was calm and collected. A stark contrast to her first meeting with Frankie D. in the makeup room of the GAP shoot.

"Oh, yeah... Yeah, my pleasure." He disregarded the topic like it was the last thing on his mind. Estelle's reflection in the mirror glanced over at him, just with her eyes. *I'm sure it was...*

"We're all set with lighting out here, so just come out to set when you're finished."

He left the room. Estelle turned her eyes back to the mirror and stared straight at herself for a full minute.

***

The set consisted of a Victorian-era styled couch, with red drapes hanging behind it. It wasn't complete yet, but would be finalized for the real shoot the next day. Estelle had been tucked into a huge couture dress, avant-garde and heavy. The color was a similar shade to that of the red drapes behind her.

She posed expertly, making love to Frankie D.'s camera. She was giving him gold. Everything looked great. With a smiling nod, he stepped back and handed the camera to his assistant.

"Alright, let's save these photos and make sure the settings and exposure are exactly the same for tomorrow."

His assistant replied quickly. "Copy that."

"Stelle, amazing. That's a wrap for today guys."

Back in the makeup room Estelle wiped the last of the thick makeup from her face and scrubbed the red lipstick from her lips. As she finished getting dressed the glam squad had their handbags over their arms as they headed out the door.

"Bye, Stelle. See you tomorrow!"

"Yeah, see you!"

As she packed her things into her tote, she pushed her hand down to the bottom of the bag and rummaged around, bringing her hand back out with a lone Reese's cup and a pack of gum. The peanut butter cup must have fallen out of the pack she had stashed in the tote. She took a piece of gum, popped it into her mouth, and threw the rest back.

When she stepped out of the makeup room, she saw Frankie D. sitting alone in the studio, going over the day's photos on his laptop. Curiosity overtook her, and she made her way to him, peeping over his shoulder.

He turned in his chair to face her. "These are gonna look incredible tomorrow once we have the rest of the set design finished. You look stunning with the red on red." He took a moment to look her over, noting her tote bag over her shoulder. "So, you heading home?"

"Yeah... Probably just gonna do my skin-care, and call it an early night. I wanna look the best I can for the actual shoot tomorrow."

"You nervous? I mean, it's the real deal tomorrow... Vogue."

She nodded, but felt confident. "Of course... But those pictures look really fantastic already. So, I'm sure it'll look even better once you have the whole set finished."

He nodded casually, his eyes only leaving her body to gaze up at her face. "I mean, it's still relatively early. You don't have to go home right away, do you?"

He reached for Estelle's hand but was barely able to graze it before she jerked it away.

"Yeah, no. I think I should. Tomorrow's really important for me."

"Come on. Stay and relax for a bit. We can... you know... have a little fun."

Estelle dreaded this same old scene with him. Maybe this time, since she was already in the shoot, he'd back off a bit.

"Yeah, I—I'm really tired..."

She wasn't so lucky. He tilted his head with narrowed eyes. "You know, if Sofie were here, she'd be a lot more grateful to me for this opportunity. And word is, she can't seem to book any new gigs. Now, hypothetically... if I called her and asked if she'd be willing to take your spot tomorrow, you think she'd be interested?"

You motherfucker... There was no fighting this man. He would find a way to threaten her every time, no matter what she gave or didn't give him. She racked her brain, desperately trying to find a way out.

"No, it's just—look, I'm on my period, okay? There."

He knew she was lying. With a smirk, his eyes dropped to her lips. "Well, I think you better put on your favorite shade of lipstick then."

Estelle sighed, closing her eyes in annoyance when he changed tactics.

"Tell you what... Take five. Go to the restroom, freshen up a bit, and think about it. If you come back out with red on those pretty little lips, I'll know you're serious about having a modeling career. If you don't..." he shrugged, "...you can go back to school and make your daddy proud by studying game theory, right?"

Estelle scoffed, so tired of his games, but she had no way out of it. She turned to head for the restroom. Frankie D. smiled devilishly and began casually rubbing himself through his pants as he watched her go.

In the restroom, Estelle entered through the door with a bang and dropped her tote on the countertop. She pulled in a long, shaky breath and stared at herself in the mirror.

Is this going to happen every time with him?

She knew the answer was, without a doubt, *yes.*

With a clenched jaw, she leaned onto the counter and looked down, thinking. Suddenly, something in her mind clicked. She quickly sifted through her tote, suddenly pausing with something in her hand, and took a deep, steadying breath.

She'd made her decision.

She stepped out of the restroom to a sight that caused sore eyes: Frankie D. was completely naked, sitting on the Victorian couch, fully erect and stroking himself.

Walking over calmly, Estelle puckered up her lips, which now had a fresh coat of red lipstick on them.

His eyes darkened as he watched her. "You made the wise decision…"

He pulled her body closer, feeling her every curve and planting kisses on her neck. She stood still, remaining blank and stoic until she lifted her hands to his shoulders, giving him a gentle push so he would lean back against the couch.

She slowly dropped down to her knees, and he spread his legs open wider as his breathing grew heavy, like a dog in heat. She lowered her head into his crotch, and slid her lips over him, taking his erection into her mouth.

Frankie D.'s eyes rolled upward as he felt the pleasure. *I'm in heaven… This is pure ecstasy…*

However, his high was short-lived. His expression suddenly changed from elated to wide-eyed and shocked.

Holy shit! What the fuck is happening?

Terror pierced his eyes and swelled the veins in his neck. He started to freak out as Estelle stood and calmly looked down at him before drooling out a mouth full of Reese's chocolatey, peanut-buttery goodness.

She spat all the gooey leftovers at him, then pulled her phone out of her pocket and began recording him as his body went into anaphylactic shock.

With a constricted throat, he desperately begged her for help. "Epi—my Epi—EpiPen… Pants… My EpiPen!"

"I know what you did to me the other night. Did you think cleaning up would make me forget? You thought

I'd think it was all some kinda dream? You better listen carefully because this is what you're gonna be doing for *me*. You're gonna book me for every—"

Estelle reluctantly cut herself short as something within her flashed red. It didn't feel right. *Why not?*

Suddenly, her mind threw memories at her. First, after she sprained her ankle, her argument with Christian: *"You are so selfish and ungrateful, you know that?"*

Her last conversation with Sam: *"It was always about you and your modeling..."*

Her last FaceTime call with Lily: *"If he's really a predator, drugging and raping girls, you can help put a stop to this. Think about how many lives he's probably destroyed and how many girls you might just save from him..."*

She closed her eyes. Controlling her rage, she sighed and shook her head. *This isn't just about me...*

"No." She opened her eyes.

As Frankie D. continued spasming, she grabbed his pants from the floor and found the EpiPen. She stabbed his thigh with it, and he gasped a huge sigh of relief as the epinephrine coursed through his body and his throat opened up again.

"You know what? If I even hear that you're still photographing girls—let alone drugging and raping them—I'll make sure everyone in the world sees this and witnesses what a creepo you *really* are. God, I wouldn't even be surprised if you just killed yourself, you pussy. And if you think I'm bluffing, show up tomorrow. I fucking dare you..."

Still recovering with spasms shooting through his body, he watched her and took in every word.

"You better call in sick right now and have Anna Wintour announce your retirement 'cause your career is over... Do I make myself clear?"

She certainly had, but Frankie D. continued to stare back defiantly. Without waiting for an answer—she didn't give him the satisfaction—she turned and headed out the door, closing it with a loud slam that rang painfully through Frankie D.'s ears.

Chapter 14:

In Vogue

"What do you mean he can't make it?" Anna Wintour frowned angrily at her assistant, Jenny. They were standing in the offices of Vogue on Madison Avenue, early in the morning. Anna had just arrived and Jenny swiftly informed her of the before-sun-up call she'd received from Frankie D., stating that he would not be making it to the shoot.

"He said… He said that—that he decided to go on vacation…"

"What?"

"In the Maldives…"

"What?" Anna stared at her, too dumbfounded to ask much else. "Vacation? The Mal—get him on my fucking line now!"

She swirled around, about to sit down behind her desk when her assistant lifted a nervous finger. "Um… I think… he turned off his phone."

"You've got to be kidding me."

"Um… no…"

"He was obviously lying, you fucking idiot! Do you genuinely believe he would go on holiday the day we're to be shooting the September issue? Honestly, you're truly dumber than I thought you were, you know that? Find out the real reason he's gone off-grid." Jenny stood, frozen, and Anna looked at her incredulously. *"Now!"*

"Okay," she quickly replied, but with one foot out of the office, Anna stopped her.

"Jenny!"

She turned around, "Yes?"

"Why don't I already have a list of other photographers to consider?"

"A list… Right. Uh… I'll have that over to you ASAP."

The confused Jenny, unsure whether she needed to find Frankie D. or his replacement, hurried to her own desk and quickly shot out a desperate email to her network of assistants in the city.

I need the best available photographers in the city, right now!

***

The camera flashed without pause while Estelle's eyes remained unblinking. She was regal, powerful, and confident in her theatrical, billowing red dress as she lay across the red Victorian couch that sat before tumbles of dramatic red drapes.

In front of her a young, female photographer moved around expertly, urging Estelle on as she snapped picture after picture, hungry for more. To the sides of the set were models, crew members, and Vogue representatives who sat in chairs behind monitors. They had oat milk lattes from Starbucks in hand, while the models' eyes were glued to their phones. Crew members silently watched the monitors, waiting for their cues to rush over and tweak whatever needed to be tweaked.

"Estelle, can we have you standing in front of the couch now? Thanks." The photographer asked.

Kelly, the key stylist on set, appeared next to her holding eight-inch designer heels, asking, "For this standing position, do you wanna see her with these on?"

She watched as Estelle stood from the couch and noticed that the dress was long enough to cover her feet completely. After a moment of thought, she looked back at Kelly. "Hmmm, you know what? Stand by, Kels. Let's do without them for now and see what we get."

"Copy. Just lemme know." Kelly nodded and stood back, while the photographer continued guiding Estelle through her next set of poses.

At the monitors, one of the Vogue reps asked another, "What happened to Frankie D.?"

"Think he called in sick. I don't know though. He seemed fine yesterday."

A third rep leaned in, "I heard Anna saying something—" his eyes landed on the recent shot of Estelle on the monitor. "Oh, wow… That's beautiful…"

The bored models looked up from their phones at the monitors when they heard that. Their gazes landed on the image of the year—Estelle, standing proud as she stared straight into the camera lens. She looked empowered, confident, and exuded the essence and attitude of a 90s supermodel. It was magical to witness.

Epilogue

Vogue—the September issue of 2021. Estelle's flawless face dominated the cover of this editorial with the words: *Estelle Li on her struggles, being Asian-American in fashion, her collapse on the runway, and rise to Top Model.*

A pair of hands flipped the magazine open and paged straight to the spread of Estelle. Each image of her was powerful and inspiring, showing her wide variety of poses, expressions, and a few in-action pictures that portrayed her humane smiles and thoughtful glances.

"Pfft."

On the page opposite a striking close-up image of her face, was a quote from Estelle's interview, captioned in bold letters: "You have to do what you have to do to get to the top. Just don't ever lose who you truly are in the process."

Seriously? Is that a joke?

The magazine slammed shut, revealing the hands of the owner. They're slim, milky and petite, with a lone tattoo on the right wrist of a Chinese character: 蔡

It was Sofie Tsai. Her eyes could have burned holes through the pages. Her once sweet and innocent gaze was now hardened into an icy-cold stare, as the thoughts in her mind culminated into one, telling statement:

This is war, bitch.

Author Bio

Adam Jay Ung is an author of dark, contemporary dramas and fiction thrillers. He has over a decade's worth of experience working behind the camera on film, TV, and commercial projects in the entertainment industry.

Some of his interests include Japanese design aesthetics, Korean music, movies, and TV shows, unsweetened Jasmine green and passion fruit teas, iced Americanos, and watching movies on the big screen. He also received his Bachelor's degree in Communication with a Minor in Film Studies from the University of California San Diego.

You can find him on Instagram @a.jay.u or on his website at www.adamjayung.com